G-R-E-E-N-E

G-R-E-E-N-E

In Praise of G-R-E-E-N-E

The author has a heartwarming way of taking her readers through school days and family events. This tale is populated with loving families, who set a good example for young readers and provide educational tidbits, too. It is told conversationally and with compassion for all.

> – Sheila Lowe, MS, CFDE, author of the *Claudia Rose Forensic Handwriting Suspense* novels

• • •

G-R-E-E-N-E is a very surprising read. This book is about three young teen girls that have grown up together in a fairly small town and how they navigate through an accidental discovery from a conversation that one of the girls overheard.

"Typical teen read," you might say. Well yes, but very different in many ways. The author takes you through their typical teen days of school, but the mystery lies with the overheard conversation and how this group of friends work through how to solve the mystery involving another girl and how to help her.

One of the most interesting aspects of this book is how the author weaves in education along with the story. I have read many books over the years, but this was a very enjoyable first. The author added vocabulary lessons and book reviews that the girls were learning during their time in school. Very different and as I traversed through the book, I found I really enjoyed the educational aspect.

You really need to read the book to appreciate it and learn something along the way. I highly recommend this not only for the teen group but to anyone that enjoys a well-written mystery.

> – Valerie Harpham, financial systems analyst for a major U.S. film studio

• • •

This story is an excellent reminder to us all not to jump to conclusions, especially when we recognize we lack all the facts.

I was grateful for the mature way the girls handled their mission to discover more information before jumping headlong into a situation they did not have all the facts for.

Getting to know all the characters was enjoyable. It was also refreshing to see how they interacted with each other.

Overall, a good read.

> – Sharon Whirledge, preschool administrator and teacher at La Petite Academy

• • •

G-R-E-E-N-E is a very interesting teen mystery because of the way Aldrete has woven her unique combination of the girls' intense curiosity with cultural situations, history lessons, medical life issues, and moral choices.

This book is packed full of fun turns in the road. I found it fascinating and an enjoyable read.

> – Linda Ankney, community relations specialist at The Artesian of Ojai

G-R-E-E-N-E

A NOVEL

BY ELAINE CLARK ALDRETE

MISSION POINT PRESS

G-R-E-E-N-E

Cover design by Andrew Kinser
Edited by Deborah DeNicola

To contact the author, please go to: Teaching Life Choices, Inc. at teachinglifechoice.org

Teaching Life Choices, Inc.

ISBN: 978-1-954786-41-7
Library of Congress Number: 2021913459

Published by Mission Point Press
2554 Chandler Rd.
Traverse City, MI 49696
(231) 421-9513
www.MissionPointPress.com

For Jacob ...
Although you may have gotten this message, I hope that you will not stop texting me for advice.

*"Being a teenager is an amazing time and a hard time. It's
when you make your best friends — I have girls who will
never leave my heart and I still talk to. You get the best and
the worst as a teen. You have the best friendships and the
worst heartbreaks."*

–SOPHIA BUSH

TABLE OF CONTENTS

ONE

TOO MUCH CANDY

*O*uch! Jen feels a sharp pain in her stomach. She can barely focus on what her teacher Mrs. Collins is saying. Something about the new book she was just reading over the weekend about the Spanish flu epidemic in 1918. *Okay, it's not the flu, but something is wrong. Maybe it was the three Eggos with lots of butter and maple syrup that I ate for breakfast.* Usually, that would not make her feel sick. But there was also the rushing around getting ready for school and mindlessly munching on a few too many Hershey's miniature candy bars. *Oh yeah, maybe I ate too much candy.*

Her friend Kendall, a red-haired, greenish-eyed girl, passes her a note asking her if she is okay, noticing she looks white as chalk. Mrs. Collins, their English teacher spots the hand-off.

"I saw that, Kendall. Would you like to share with the rest of the class?"

Kendall rolls her eyes, sighs, and says, "Jen looks sick, Mrs. C."

Mrs. Collins, who loves her role as an English arts teacher, exposing students to new and unusual words and classics of juvenile fiction, looks over at Jen and says, "You do look pale, Jennifer—do you want to visit the nurse?"

Jen really wants nothing less than to go to the nurse's office, a disgusting place that usually smells of vomit. At the same time, if she is going to be sick, she would rather not barf in class in front of everybody. How humiliating that would be!

Feeling too shaky to talk, Jen just nods. Mrs. Collins gestures towards the door and begins describing the books that the students will get to choose from. As Jen leaves the room, Mrs. Collins is pitching *The Grapes of Wrath* written by John Steinbeck. She says, "The book won a Pulitzer Prize for fiction!"

As Jen walks down the hall towards the nurse's office she decides to stop at the bathroom. Built in the 1950s, this side of the school is the oldest. It has single-person bathrooms, not like the larger, multiple-stall bathrooms in the newer part of the school. The mirror is not glass, but polished metal, with tiny scratches in it. She sticks her tongue out and hears a gurgle in her stomach. A wave of nausea comes over her and she almost loses her balance.

Jen realizes that her legs are shaky, so it takes her several minutes to walk down the hallway. In the small nurse's office, Ms. Heather is on the phone and she holds her finger up to Jen indicating for her to wait.

Ms. Heather is neither dressed in scrubs nor business attire. She prefers dressy casual, which makes her feel less like a nurse and more like a member of the educational team. She teaches most of the health-related classes. Of course, she is responsible for dispensing prescription medicines and caring for the students who come to her office feeling ill. But it makes no sense to dress up because at least once a month she ends up with vomit on her blouse or pants. When she looks up at Jen, the thought that she might need her extra set of clothes quickly crosses her mind.

"You look pasty, dear," she says.

"Yeah," Jen says, as she puts her hand on her stomach. "I don't feel very well at all."

Ms. Heather picks up her pen and asks, "It's Jennifer, correct?"

Jen simply nods.

"What is your last name, please?"

"Benson."

Jen watches Ms. Heather as she fills in her name on the form. Ms. Heather gets up from her chair and motions for Jen to follow her into a room behind the small front office. Motioning towards a hospital examining room with a cot, Ms. Heather says, "Please sit down, I want to take your temperature." Ms. Heather places the thermometer under Jen's tongue until it makes the usual beeping sound.

"Okay, 99.1, that's normal. How long have you been feeling sick?"

"I don't know, maybe about an hour."

"Go ahead and lie down."

Jen sits on the cot, lifts her legs, turns her body, and lays her head on the pillow.

"Do you want me to call one of your parents?"

"I don't think so, not yet. I might feel better in a few minutes."

Ms. Heather turns, starting to leave the room, stops, and asks, "Oh, and where is the note from your teacher?"

It is school policy for students to have a note whenever

they are not in class. Jen should have had a hall pass. She looks up at Ms. Heather and answers, "I don't have one."

"Whose class did you come from?" Ms. Heather lets out a heavy sigh.

"Mrs. Collins, I came from Mrs. Collins' class."

"I should have known," Ms. Heather says, quietly, sort of under her breath.

Jen looks up at her, confused, not sure if she was supposed to answer or even if she should have heard.

"Pardon me?"

Ms. Heather looks down at Jen, realizing the awkwardness of the moment. She pats Jen's shoulder and says "That's fine; I'll come back in about ten minutes to check on you. Does that sound okay?"

"That sounds good, thank you."

Ms. Heather walks back to her desk leaving the door half-open. Jen can see her hands as she begins writing something on her chart.

Jen has brown eyes, and light brown hair—although some refer to it as dirty-blond—which reaches just below her shoulders. Her parents describe her as a future heartbreaker. Today she is wearing her favorite red Old Navy shirt and a new pair of faded blue jeans. Since she did not have gym class today, she isn't wearing socks, just a pair of black-and-white checkered Vans. Jen begins to trace her finger over the seam of her jeans. As she moves her fingers up and down in a mesmerizing rhythm, she drifts off to sleep.

❧

When Jen slowly wakes up, she's totally unaware of how long

she has been asleep. It could have been a few minutes or an hour. She has no clue. Her father sometimes falls asleep while watching TV. He is known to sleep through most of a show and awaken with a bewildered look on his face. She thinks that she is like her father in some ways. But right now, she feels disorientated.

As she wipes her eyes, she can hear voices in the nurse's office. One is obviously Ms. Heather, and the other is a girl. Suddenly Jen hears something that brings her completely awake.

"I've been high all day," the girl says.

Jen believes that the word "high" has to do with drugs. It is not like she has ever taken any drugs herself. But she has taken a drug-awareness class and knows what drugs are and even what certain drugs do. Her friend Emma has an older brother who has caused their family a lot of heartache and trouble because he was involved with drugs—the illegal kind. She knows that drugs are really bad news and hearing some-body around her age say that they have been high all day is very startling.

Jen sits up and tries to see through the half-open door. But all she can see is Ms. Heather's desk. She twists her neck to get a better look. The girl is wearing black Converse shoes and anxiously tapping her feet.

"Are you high right now?" Ms. Heather asks.

"Yes," the girl says in a distressed tone.

"Alright," Ms. Heather says calmly. "Let's check again in about an hour to see if you are still high."

"Okay, okay," the girl says with a heavy sigh.

"I know that you understand," Jen overhears Ms. Heather say as she hears her chair move.

Jen can see Ms. Heather standing in the doorway. "I realize that you hate reporting to me, but you are working with a serious drug, and we want you to be safe."

"I know," the girl says with another heavy sigh.

Jen hears the girl stand up from the chair and walk away from Ms. Heather. Jen strains to see who the black Converse belong to but all she can see is the bottom of a black backpack with bright orange piping on the edges.

Ms. Heather turns and looks in at Jen who is now sitting up. She asks, "Jennifer, how are you feeling?"

Jen has almost forgotten why she is there. She blinks a couple of times and realizes that she feels better. "I'm feeling a whole lot better," she says, sounding surprised.

"Well enough to go back to class?" Ms. Heather asks.

"I think so," Jen says as she swings her legs around, puts her feet on the floor, and carefully stands up. She places her hand on her stomach. Nothing happens.

"Yup, I'm all good," she says.

Ms. Heather walks around her desk and picks up a clipboard. Jen can see that her name is on it with a space for check-in time, which reads 9:50, and in the space for check-out time, Ms. Heather writes 10:35.

"Wow, I was asleep for almost an hour?" Jen asks.

"Yes, yes you were, and it seems to have been just the remedy."

Jen looks down at the list again and sees that there is a name right under her own. It only has a check-in time of 10:25. She imagines that this is High Girl. She tries to read the name without being too obvious. The first name is smudged and unreadable. All that she can read is the last name, Greene.

Hmm, who do I know with the last name of Greene? This information is too sketchy to figure out who High Girl is.

Ms. Heather realizes that Jen's eyes are lingering a little too long on the list and she covers it with her arm. These are confidential records. No student should see another's information. Ms. Heather puts the clipboard on her lap, reaches into her drawer, and takes out a hall pass, a yellow three-by-five card. She hands it to Jen.

"Do you know where your next class is?"

"Yes, it's with Mr. Jackson."

"Give this to him and please ask him to return it to me soon because I'm running low on them."

"I will and thank you."

Jen walks towards the door and hears Ms. Heather say, "I'm happy that you are feeling better!" Jen gives a wave over her shoulder without really looking back.

She walks past Mrs. Collins' classroom and towards Mr. Jackson's room. She is not really thinking about the portion of classes that she has missed while resting in the nurse's office. Or even the reason that she was there. She is suddenly worried about High Girl but also a little angry. She has seen what drugs can do to the person taking them and to their family. Now, this girl is bringing drugs into her school! She realizes that she is angry with Ms. Heather as well because she had acted so nonchalantly.

Nonchalant—one of Mrs. Collins' unusual words that means relaxed and calm in a way that shows that you do not care or are not worried about anything. Jen thinks that she has used the word correctly. Ms. Heather should have been shocked. She knows bringing drugs to school is a serious offense.

Ms. Heather should have lectured that girl. Instead, she

almost seemed to be encouraging her to take drugs! This is very strange; there must be some reason. But I cannot figure out what it could be. I have to talk to Kendall and Emma about this and the sooner the better.

TWO

LET IT OUT!

Jen cannot wait for her lunch period. She just has to tell Kendall and Emma what she heard Ms. Heather say to High Girl. Although the three girls have a class together and actually sit near one another, they aren't going to be able to talk. Mr. Jackson is not in a very good mood today! Of course, Jen has missed the first part of the class, but she can tell that a good deal of the students did not do well on their most recent quiz.

Mr. Jackson is of average height and build; he has blue eyes and neatly trimmed blonde hair. He usually wears a white dress shirt with the sleeves rolled up and brown or black slacks. Most students know that he wears contact lenses because at times during the school year he will wear a pair of glasses. He is friendly and kind, yet firm with his grading process.

When Mr. Jackson sees Jen come in, he takes the hall pass from her and motions for her to take her seat. He is pointing out what he has written on the board. He then walks over to his desk, picks up a paper, and takes it to Jen. It is her quiz and she sees at the top of the page in red pencil that her grade is ninety-three percent. She is pleased with that score. Knowing that she has done so well, she stops listening and begins wondering about the girl from Ms. Heather's office. *Last name Greene, black Converse, black backpack, orange piping ... .*

By the time class is nearly over, most of the problems that Mr. Jackson had written on the board have been correctly solved. Mr. Jackson seems a lot less annoyed. Just before the bell rings, he says that he will not be quizzing the students on this specific material again, although he will be adding a few more difficult problems on their next quiz. As he does each day, he announces that he will be available after school for anyone who feels that they need help. Finally, the bell rings for lunch.

According to school policy hats are only allowed to be worn before or after school and at lunch period. A couple of the boys open their backpacks and take out caps. One is Tommy. He takes out his University of Arizona cap. Jen is not yet really into boys that much but thinks that Tommy is kind of cute.

Emma comes up behind Jen and puts her hand on Jen's shoulder. This startles Jen a little. "Like what you see? Take a picture, it'll last longer," Emma says.

Jen turns and smiles at Emma. Emma uses a lot of funny phrases like that. They are probably things that she has seen on the Internet or from watching TV for hours and hours. "Yeah right!" Jen says as she picks up her backpack and puts her arms through the straps to get it onto her back.

Emma Perez is pretty; Jen will admit, privately, that she is the prettiest of her friends. Emma's family is Argentinian. Although her parents have traditional names; Julieta and Franco, they wanted Emma to be more Americanized. Emma has her mom's jet-black hair, and her skin has an everlasting tan. She is fully Americanized, from her love of pizza and hot dogs to Mickey Mouse and all things Disney to the iPhone that she has in the inner pocket of her backpack.

Last year one of the older boys called Emma "exotic." But what does that mean exactly? She has looked the same her whole life. She thinks that she is completely normal and not exotic. Technically, the word exotic means a characteristic unusually different and attractive or originating in a distant foreign country. If you are from Argentina and live in the United States, you would be exotic. Jen thinks that that boy meant that Emma is exceptionally beautiful. And Jen agrees.

"Okay, what is so earthshaking?" Kendall asks as the three girls walk together towards the cafeteria.

"Yeah, tell us, tell us!" Emma shouts, as she leaves Kendall's side and moves in next to Jen so that she can hear her better.

"Once we sit down, I will tell you everything," Jen says.

Kendall is always ready to hear a story about someone's adventure or any kind of challenge. She looks a little let down. Emma, however, is ready to eat. She holds up her lunch bag for Jen and Kendall to see, and says, "Look, I have Mama's meatloaf today!" with a huge smile. This is meatloaf on white bread with ketchup. Jen does not really like meatloaf the way her own mother makes it. But Mrs. Perez's meatloaf is delicious, and Jen feels a little jaundiced.

Jaundiced—another one of Mrs. Collins' unusual words, meaning exhibiting or influenced by envy.

Both of Jen's parents work full-time jobs; they do not send her to school with a homemade lunch. As they enter the cafeteria the girls split up. Emma and Kendall go to their usual table and Jen gets into the line. Today, her choices are a hamburger with fries, pineapple glazed turkey with mashed potatoes, or pizza. Despite the earlier stomachache, Jen opts for the pizza. She adds a carton of apple juice. All these items go on her lunch account. Jen's parents pay monthly for her to eat the cafeteria meals.

Jen doesn't want to tell her friends, but she rather likes the three options to choose from each day. The lunches that they are having are fine, but she knows that they are probably last night's leftovers. She doesn't like leftovers much.

When Jen gets to their table Emma has eaten nearly half of her meatloaf sandwich. Kendall has poured chicken noodle soup from her thermos into the cup and is sipping it.

Kendall Murphy's family is Irish and English. She once told Jen that they could trace their family origin on her father's side back to the 1800s. Kendall gets her red hair from her father, Liam. Liam is short for William which means "helmet of will" and strong-willed warrior. Kendall's mother, Kate, traces her heritage back to England. Kendall's name translates to Kircabikendala; meaning village with a church in the valley of the Kent river. The earliest recorded form of this town's name was in 1095. Jen is very happy that Kendall's parents chose the much shorter version as she is positive that she would never be able to spell or say the original version.

Emma takes another bite of her sandwich. She tries to be patient. "Alright, let it out!" she blurts out as soon as Jen sits down.

"Wait just a minute," Jen says. "The last time I talked at lunch, I didn't get to eat anything!"

This is true; the last time was when Jen had overheard that Mr. Jackson was going to Hawaii for his Honeymoon. It had not been common knowledge that he was even getting married. They had talked about whether he would continue to teach or perhaps move away. They knew that people some-times move away after they marry. They all like Mr. Jackson and think that he is pretty fair when it comes to grades. Of course, Mr. Jackson didn't end up moving away.

This news was *much* bigger though!

Even though Jen is not that hungry she doesn't want to faint in the middle of French Class with Madame Bebeau. Madame Bebeau, a short woman with black hair and blue eyes, received her bachelor's degree from Queens College, Master's degree, and a doctorate in French linguistics from Indiana University. She is obviously smart and well prepared, but she drones on and on in conjugating verbs and Jen sometimes feels she will fall asleep in her class. But Jen reasons, falling asleep is preferable to fainting.

Knowing all the trouble that Emma's brother, Jimmy, has caused Emma and her family, Jen is worried about her. Jimmy had been high on drugs during the spring and attempted to rob a convenience store. He was restricted to their home all summer, except to go to work and home. Their mother had to drive him because he was arrested while driving and had his license revoked. His trial was late in the summer, and he agreed to plead guilty to DUI (driving under the influence), then he had to go to jail. Emma had been very withdrawn for the first few weeks of school and Jen really doesn't want to say anything that will cause her to be so introverted and distant again.

Yet this story must be told.

"So, I was in Ms. Heather's office." Of course, Kendall already knows this because she told Mrs. C that Jen was sick.

"I fell asleep, surprisingly, for almost an hour," Jen says. "Anyways, when I woke up Ms. Heather was talking to a girl."

"What's so unusual about that?" asks Emma.

Jen leans in close to Emma and Kendall and whispers

loudly, "The girl said that she was high and had been all morning!"

"No way!" Kendall almost shouts.

"Uhm yes, I heard the conversation!"

"Who was it?" asks Emma.

"I really don't know, I tried to see, but the door was only half-open. All I could see was her black Converse and backpack," says Jen.

"Nothing else?" asks Kendall.

"Nope, then Ms. Heather told her to come back in about an hour to see if she was still high. I don't get it!" Jen whispers.

Emma has put her sandwich down and is staring at Jen. What is so weird is that Ms. Heather had given them "the talk" when they took her Drug Awareness class ... but is she encouraging someone to take drugs now? How can this be?

"Who was the girl?" asks Emma as if she had not heard Jen's answer just seconds ago.

"I told you, I don't know. She is not in any of our classes. I'm not even sure what grade she is in. But I did see her last name."

"What is it?" Emma and Kendall both chime in.

"It's Greene, spelled with an E at the end."

THREE

THE LAYLA CONNECTION

The rest of the day goes pretty much as any other school day. Jen goes to her French, Earth Science, Intro to Computers, and U.S. History classes. Once the last bell rings the girls meet and walk towards home together, stopping at the elementary school to pick up Jen's little sister Layla.

All three families have lived in the same neighborhood for as long as the girls can remember. Hacienda Acres is one of those central neighborhoods that outsiders do not expect. It has turn-of-the-century traditional-style houses and mission-style bungalows painted in browns, turquoise, and sage greens sitting on quiet tree-lined streets, all within walking distance to school, shops, and parks. Named after an early civic leader, the neighborhood is in a constant state of revitalization as new homeowners move in to restore older homes. It is a cross-section of the town with everyone from university professors to starving students, lawyers, and civic leaders to artists, young families to sports stars living there. Jen and Kendall live next door to each other, and Emma lives four houses down.

The four girls walk the short distance to their neighborhood, where they leave Emma at her house. Emma says, "Just give me five minutes and I'll be at your house, Jen." Jen knows that it will be more like ten minutes, but that is okay.

Kendall takes off running to her house to get her last yearbook.

Once Jen and Layla are home, they put their backpacks down and Jen goes to her room to find her last yearbook. The plan is, once they are all together, to look through the pages of each grade to see if they can find anyone with the last name Greene.

Kendall and Emma arrive at about the same time. They all sit down at the dining room table and begin flipping through the pages of their yearbooks. There are so many students that they are surprised to realize how many that they do not know. On a page of twenty-five photos, Jen admits that she only knows two.

Kendall shows Emma and Jen a picture of Jacob Anderson. Jacob is a sandy-haired, blue-eyed boy, who plays football on both the varsity and junior varsity teams. He is charming, easy to talk to and friendly to everyone. Most of his friends think that he is outgoing, witty, and smart. He is always quick with a smile.

"Isn't he just the cutest?" Kendall kind of coos.

"I guess, if you say so," replies Jen with a little wink and a smile which makes Kendall begin to blush a little bit.

Emma holds up a page and says, "Remember Tracey Adams?"

Jen and Kendall shake their heads in agreement. Tracey had lived three streets over. But during the summer she had had to move to Maryland because her grandparents were both incapable of living on their own and her mom had no other family there to assist with their care.

After about ten minutes they have not found one student named Greene. In a frustrated tone, Jen says, "What we really need is this year's yearbook." But of course, it has not been printed yet.

Kendall says, "We should try a Google search." She takes

her iPad out of her backpack. Not realizing how common the name Greene is, and surprisingly, there are a lot of famous people with the last name Greene.

Kendall reads aloud, "Examples of famous people include Ashley Greene, Joe Greene and Lorne Greene. Ashley Greene is an American Actress and model, best known for playing Alice Cullen in the *Twilight* films. Joe Greene, also known as "Mean Joe," is a former all-pro American football defensive tackle who played for the Pittsburg Steelers from 1969-1981. He is widely considered to be one of the best defensive linemen to play in the NFL. Lorne Greene was a Canadian actor who was best known for his role as Ben Cartwright on the western *Bonanza* and Commander Adama on *Battlestar Galactica*." This, of course, is of no help in finding the Greene that they are looking for, but interesting all the same.

Layla has been listening to Kendall and her friends mulling over the Google information and she suddenly says quite matter-of-factly, "I know a girl named Connie Greene. She probably isn't famous though."

All three girls' heads quickly turn around to look at Layla almost causing them to have whiplash.

"What did you say, Layla?!" Jen squeals.

"I know a girl named Connie Greene."

"Is it spelled G-r-e-e-n-e?" Kendall asks.

"I have no idea. Why?"

"Can you ask her if she has an older sister at our school?" Emma asks.

"Okay, I guess. Can I watch TV now?"

"Sure, if your homework is done," Jen replies.

Jen and Emma are both taking French. Kendall has decided to take Spanish to be different. Kendall's mom works an earlier shift to be home by 4:30. Usually, after Kendall's mom gets home, she goes home to finish her homework and helps prepare dinner.

Jen and Emma leave Layla to watch TV.

"Elle mange une salade. That means she eats salad," Emma says.

"Nous aimons la musique. That means we love music."

"Ils aiment jouer. That means they like to play."

And so back and forth they go, bouncing the phrases that they have been studying. It almost seems more like a fun game rather than actually studying. They have done this sort of game-style studying for many of their subjects as far back as Jen can remember. And it does pay off!

When Jen's mom gets home, Emma leaves, yelling, "Au revoir!" as she scoots out the door.

It is Layla's turn to set the table for dinner this week and Jen calls her into the kitchen to do her chore. Jen will be helping with slicing the vegetables for the salad. Their mom has decided on pizza. She takes a frozen crust from the freezer, places it on her Pampered Chef pizza stone, and begins pouring the sauce on it. She adds pepperoni slices and tops it off with shredded cheese. Jen decides not to mention that she had pizza for lunch. Her mom works so hard and comes home to make dinner every night too. Besides, her stomachache is gone.

"How are you doing with the salad, Jen?" asks her mom.

"Everything is almost ready."

"Layla, is the table set? Dad should be pulling into the driveway any minute."

The Benson family always sits in the dining room for family dinners. As they eat, they talk about their days. Their dad starts with "So did anything exciting happen today?"

"I wouldn't exactly call it exciting, but I wasn't feeling very well so Mrs. Collins sent me to Ms. Heather's office. I was there for about an hour. Then I felt well enough to go back to class."

"Why do you suppose that you weren't feeling well?" Jen's mom asks, with a look of concern.

Jen begins, "Well, I'm not sure but I'm good now."

"Maybe you ate too much candy," Layla interrupts.

"It's none of your business Layla!" Jen shoots back.

Neither of their parents likes it very much when the girls argue. It has been a long day for both at work. All they really want is a nice peaceful evening. Although it does not happen often, it is frustrating. Both Jen's parents tell her that she should not be eating candy in the morning and that is that. Jen had thought about telling her parents about the girl in Ms. Heather's office but the little squabble between her and Layla causes her to forget.

After dinner, Jen helps her mom with clearing the table then loads the dishes into the dishwasher as her mom washes the pizza stone by hand. Her dad is going over math homework with Layla. Layla likes math and is good at it too.

Per the Benson family house rules, the girls are only allowed to watch two programs on TV. They usually watch game shows such as *Wheel of Fortune* or *Jeopardy*. Then it will be time for brushing their teeth, getting into pajamas, reading or homework for Jen, then off to sleep. Their mom has the theory that no matter what your age, changing into pajamas can be calming and set the mood for a good bedtime routine. Layla loves her Hanna Anderson pajamas because they are so soft and on cold nights, they keep her warm. Sometimes she likes to mix and match the interchangeable tops and bottoms.

As Jen is brushing her teeth, she thinks about Layla asking her new friend Connie if she has an older sister. *Does Connie know that her sister is taking drugs? I'm sure that she would have no idea. The poor thing, I sure hope that she doesn't have to go through the trouble that Emma has had with Jimmy. That's just too hard.*

FOUR

SEARCHING FOR EG

As the girls leave Layla off at her school, Jen says, "Don't forget to ask Connie if her sister goes to our school."

"Yeah, okay, whatever," Layla shrugs.

Jen, Emma, and Kendall continue to their school. Once there, they begin to look for a girl with a black backpack with orange piping and black Converse, hoping that she is wearing the same shoes today as yesterday. However, there are so many students, the girls become discouraged. They watch as buses pull up looking over the students who get off. More students get out of their parents' car, and this is only the East side of the school. There is no sign of High Girl.

The morning classes go pretty much as usual, other than the fact that Derek is disruptive in Mrs. Collins' class. A rich kid from the Peach Hill Estates neighborhood, Derek White always dresses in the best clothes. For him, everything is a name brand like *Nike, Tommy Hilfiger, Calvin Klein,* or *H&M.*

Jen knows some families who live in Peach Hill Estates. She has been to a few birthday parties there over the years and has seen how huge those houses are. Most are two stories with five bedrooms and a bathroom for each, on two-acre lots with big driveways and mountain views. Some have a large open great room while others feature one bedroom and bath down-stairs. Jen knows that these houses are much more expensive than the ones in her neighborhood.

Derek has come into class just as the bell has rung, almost late. He has his iPod in his hand, the earbuds in his ears, and the sound up so loud that the other students can hear his music. Mrs. Collins is not happy. She immediately motions for Derek to come to her desk. She holds her hand out and with a sigh says "Okay, let me have it. You know that iPods are not allowed during class. You'll get it back after class."

"B-b-but, Mrs. C." Derek stutters as he pulls the earbuds out and hands her his iPod. He walks back to his seat and slumps down.

Of course, he is apparently trying to become invisible, Jen thinks.

At lunchtime, the girls once again gather at their usual table. Today Jen has chicken nuggets and fries with a carton of milk. Emma and Kendall have their usual lunches. In whispers, they compare notes on what they have seen during the morning.

None of them have seen anyone who particularly stood out as the possible High Girl. They have seen students with black backpacks, mostly belonging to boys and there were none with orange piping at all. There really isn't much to say regarding High Girl.

After school, Jen and Emma say their goodbyes to Kendall because she must attend her afternoon volunteering today.

Kendall is an only child. She craves Jen's relationship with Layla. She thinks that Jen has it especially good because she is the big sister. To fulfill her desire to have a relationship with younger children Kendall volunteers as a track coach for Lane 5.

Lane 5 is a city team for children between the ages of five

and eleven years old. Lane 5 is a part of a conference that has nine clubs, boys, and girls, throughout the county. Their motto is "One Dream, One Team." Some of the clubs in the conference date back to the late 1970s. The Warriors were added in 1984, the Running Rebels in 1986, and the Flying Phoenix in 2006. Kendall is responsible for training the children in the proper technique in the long jump, sprints, and the 4x100m relay. She likes the 4x100m relay the best. This sprint relay is an event run in lanes over one lap of the track with four runners completing 100 meters each. The first runners must begin in the same stagger. A stagger ensures that all runners complete the same distance during the race. A relay baton is carried by each runner.

Kendall is pleased to see the younger kids are doing particularly well today. She wants her team to earn some medals in their next track meet. They will be competing with the Running Rebels and Flying Phoenix in just over two weeks.

Jen, Emma, and Layla walk home together, as they have every day and they leave Emma at her house. Layla has said that she has something to tell the girls. But Jen told her to keep it to herself until Kendall has gotten to their house.

Jen tells Layla to sit down to do her homework. Today Layla will work on her vocabulary words. She has a list of twenty words to learn the use of. The exercise is to circle the word in each of the sentences.

A few of the words are:

Usually - They *usually* walk home together.

Character - Mickey Mouse is a cartoon *character*.

Friend - Sarah has a *friend* named Kim.

Layla works on her homework until around four o'clock when Emma comes in the back door.

"Bonjour!" Emma shouts.

"Bonjour, Kendall should be here any time now," replies Jen.

Layla excitedly asks, "Now, Jen?"

"No, not yet. Wait until Kendall gets here," Jen says.

"What do you want to drink?" Jen asks Emma.

"Water would be fine."

Jen takes out two glasses then looks over at Layla and asks if she wants a drink as well. Layla shakes her head yes. Jen takes out two more glasses anticipating that Kendall will be there soon and want a glass of water too.

Just as Jen is filling the glasses with water, Kendall comes in the back door. She is a little out of breath. "I ran over as soon as I got home," she says.

Again, Layla wants her story to be heard and says, "It's about time!"

Jen retorts, "Zip your lips Layla, or this water is going down the drain!"

"Oh Jen, let Layla talk. What do you have for us, Munchkin? Did you talk to Connie today?" Kendall asks.

Layla excitedly says, "Yes, I did!"

"So, does she have a sister at our school?" Emma asks.

"Yes, she does."

"Well, what does she look like? What color hair? How tall is she?" Jen asks.

"Connie is shorter than me. She has brown color hair and brown eyes. She was wearing a pink shirt with a fox on it and blue jeans today," Layla says proudly.

"We really need to know what her *sister* looks like, Layla," Kendall says.

"Oh, I don't know what she looks like, but I know her name."

"You do?!" Jen, Emma, and Kendall all chime in together.

"Yeah, Connie said it's Eve."

As a treat for her part in the detective work, Jen decides to allow Layla to watch TV. Layla has finished her homework, although she has not done her chores. Jen will do that for her as an extra reward.

Now they have a name. They don't know which grade she is in. They don't know what color hair and eyes she has or even how tall she is. Yet, they know that they are looking for Eve Greene. They know that they need to find her!

FIVE

WHERE TO START

"Wow, it's already Friday!" Jen says as she dances around the kitchen making her breakfast. She has decided on a banana dog; peanut butter, a banana, and raisins in a long whole-grain bun. Layla is still in her room.

Jen's mom is talking to her dad in the living room. Jeff works as a Financial Planning Manager for Edward Jones. Their motto is, "Edward Jones is an investment firm that believes your financial goals deserve face-to-face interactions to build quality relationships with our clients." Jeff has been working for the company in his current capacity for almost eight years. He had to pass certain tests to become licensed and work as an FP as he and most of his co-workers refer to themselves. He likes his job because it gives him a lot of independence. He has flexible hours and Friday is his usual work-from-home day.

Layla walks into the kitchen and says, "I'm hungry, Daddy."

"What would you like for breakfast, Pumpkin?"

"I'd like waffles, please."

Jeff goes into the kitchen, makes waffles for Layla, sets them on the table, gives her a quick kiss on the forehead, and returns to the living room to resume watching his morning news program, *Worldwide Exchange.*

Jen's mom, Robin, has already eaten a bagel and coffee and is heading out the door to her office. She is a Staff Accountant and Tax Preparer for Englander and Englander, CPAs. They are a firm located in the next town over. This is a father and son-owned company. The father, Herb, is her favorite because he always has a good story to tell. Robin likes her job but admits that some days are harder than others, especially near the end of the month or quarter. That's when there are more reports due, and she sometimes must work overtime. Robin has been with Englander and Englander since Layla started first grade.

Once Jen and Layla finish their breakfast, Jeff tells them to brush their teeth and get dressed for school, which they do. They are out the door and walking towards Kendall's house when she comes out of her side door.

"Hi! Can you believe how fast this week has gone?" Jen shouts at Kendall.

"I know. So fast that it's the weekend!" Kendall replies as they walk to meet Emma.

They have decided to refer to Eve Greene as "EG" so that they can talk about her without anyone else knowing who or what they are talking about.

When the girls are almost to Layla's school, Emma asks, "What are we going to do to figure out how to talk to EG?"

"I don't know, I guess we'll just casually ask around," Jen says.

Then Kendall offers, "That way maybe we can figure out if we know anybody in her core group. We can't find her and just walk up to her and say something like 'Hey, we know you're taking drugs—you know.'"

"Well, of course not, silly!" Emma replies.

Once in their classroom with Mrs. Collins, Jen and Kendall are focused on the books that she has assigned. Kendall has chosen *The Book Thief* by Markus Zusak and Jen decides on *The Grapes of Wrath* by John Steinbeck.

The Book Thief is a story narrated by an extremely overworked being who identifies himself as Death. He tells us about Liesel Meminger, a girl growing up in Germany during World War II. She steals books, learns to read, and finds comfort in words. She and Max, a Jewish boy, who her foster parents, Hans and Rosa, hide in their basement to protect him from the Nazis, survive the war. Books are an important part of this story, and therefore, words hold great value. In the book that Max wrote for Liesel, *The Word Shaker,* he suggests that words are the most powerful force on Earth. To Liesel, words also offer comfort and a means of escape. Words are her place of refuge while the Nazis control her world.

Kendall loves the description of Rudy. In the book, Liesel used this sentence to describe Rudy: "bony legs, gangly blue eyes, and hair the color of a lemon." Kendall imagines herself being Liesel. Rudy is her sidekick. He is academically and athletically gifted, which attracts the attention of the officials of the Nazi Party. They try to recruit him, but he wants nothing to do with them, which becomes a problem. Rudy becomes Liesel's best friend and eventually falls in love with her. He is always asking her for a kiss. The story is dramatic and romantic, but more importantly it stresses the comfort of reading books, getting lost in someone else's vision of a certain time and place. Kendall feels reading is like travelling to distant lands. Books can take you anywhere and back in time throughout history and of course, they are made of words! Words are so important because they can both express what you want to say and because they can be misunderstood. Kendall thinks about how carefully she and Jen and Emma must choose their words as they go on their detective mission to uncover EG.

The Grapes of Wrath takes place in the 1930s during America's Great Depression, which lasted from the October 1929 Stock Market crash until World War II began twelve years later. This novel focuses on the Joad family, poor tenant farmers, forced from their Oklahoma home by several unfortunate circumstances, including drought, agricultural industry changes, and finally, the banks foreclosing on their property. They feel almost hopeless; they set out for California along with thousands of other people who are referred to as "Okies," seeking a better future.

Jen is horrified by what life would possibly be like if she and her family had no food, clothing, or proper shelter. How could they live in the back of a truck for so long? And picking peaches or cotton is not her idea of work that she could see herself doing.

Kendall leans over to Jen and whispers, "Rudy reminds me of Jacob. Maybe I could ask him if he knows EG or anybody else who knows her." Kendall secretly thinks that this would give her a chance to speak to Jacob.

Jen thinks about that for a few moments and whispers, "Sure that might be a good idea. When will you see Jacob?"

"I should see him this afternoon. He usually helps with our volleyball set up and take-down."

Now they have the starting of a plan to find EG. Their big question is what they might do once they meet her. Emma may have an idea. They will be able to talk again at lunchtime. Maybe they will be able to come up with the next steps.

The morning goes by rather quickly for a Friday, which usually is painfully slow. Everybody just wants the weekend to start. There are movies to see, friends to hang out with and a person could actually sleep in late the next day!

Lunch turns out to be somewhat uneventful. The girls sit together as always. But they still do not have a plan. Well, Kendall has her plan to ask Jacob if he knows who EG is. But that's it. What will they do if Jacob knows EG? Nobody has a clue.

"So, I chose *The Book Thief*," Kendall says to Emma. "What are you going to read?"

"I thought that I had already told you that I want to read *To Kill a Mockingbird* by Harper Lee."

To Kill a Mockingbird uses memorable characters to explore civil rights and racisim in the segregated South during the 1930s. This story is told through the eyes of Scout Finch, an adventurous child who prefers the company of boys and generally solves her problems with her fists. We meet her kind-hearted but firm father, Atticus Finch, an attorney who hopelessly strives to prove the innocence of a black man, Tom Robinson, unjustly accused of beating and raping a white woman named Mayella Ewell. The story also introduces us to Boo Radley, a mysterious neighbor who saves Scout and her brother Jem from being killed. A good part of the story's genius lies in the fact that it is told from the child's point of view. The book opens with, "Lawyers, I suppose, were children once."

Emma cannot imagine solving problems with her fists like Scout. And she loves the company of her friends who are girls. They can easily talk to each other about boys. It is also hard for her to imagine not having a mother. However, the relationship of Jem and Scout in the novel is somewhat close to her own relationship with her older brother Jimmy; he has always tried to protect her too.

Before they know it, lunch period is over, and they are off to their afternoon classes.

Once school lets out, Kendall goes to the gymnasium for her volleyball game. She looks around for Jacob, but he is not there, at least not yet. She goes into the locker room and changes into her uniform. Today, they are playing against the Warden Tigers.

Although volleyball was developed in 1895 and the first World Championships were held in 1949, women were not allowed to play until 1952. Kendall loves volleyball. She's happy that she can play. She hopes that this game will bring her team one step closer to league champions.

The game is hard-fought; however, the Coyotes are defeated by a score of 3-2. Brooke G is named the "Player of the Match." She has eight assists, five aces, a serve which lands in the opponent's court without being touched, and four digs which is when a player receives an attacked ball and keeps it in play. Kendall goes over to Brooke and congratulates her on her excellent performance. Then Kendall looks around for Jacob. She must ask him if he knows EG. But what will she say if he asks her why she wants to know? She knows that she will have to come up with something quickly. She hasn't even uttered a mere "Hi" to him. She has only watched him from afar setting up and taking down the equipment for the volley-ball games. She doesn't know if he even knows who she is. But she wants him to know who she is and more importantly, she wants to know if he has any information about EG. As she looks around, she thinks ... *Where could he be? He's always here to take down the equipment.*

SIX

HOMECOMING DANCE

Jacob's mother, Abecca, and Dylan's mother, Chelsea Grey, met at work. Abecca is the Assistant to the Sales Manager. She doesn't think that it is really the best title for all that is expected of her in her position. She sets up meetings, conducts interviews of prospective employees, calculates payroll as well as arranging for the company's annual conference and golf tournament. Chelsea was originally hired as the receptionist. That changed when Chelsea was promoted to Customer Service Representative three years ago. Then near the end of the year before last, Chelsea's husband, Kevin, who works for Boeing, was transferred to Kansas.

Jacob and Dylan have been friends since they can remember. The Grey family's move was a difficult transition for both boys. They miss each other a lot. After all, they had attended pre-school through their last year of middle school together, playing on the city flag football team while in elementary school. By sharing many sleepovers, family camping and fishing trips too, they became very close.

Today Jacob plans to ask Kendall to go to the Homecoming dance. He is nervous about asking her since he has never even talked to her. But he has watched her play volleyball and he thinks that she is pretty. Hoping that she will want to go with him, he is still excited about the varsity football team who just won their last game and the Homecoming dance will be their celebration. Overall, he would like to get to know Kendall better.

He decides to call Dylan after he has finished setting up for the volleyball game. He walks outside.

"Hey dude, what's up?" Dylan asks when he answers his phone.

"Uhm, nothing much, really."

"How's football going?"

"Oh yeah, it's going great! We won this week's game, so we are league champions!" Jacob says excitedly.

"That's super awesome!"

"Yeah, and there is this girl ... um ... her name is Kendall and I ... um I want to ask her to go to the Homecoming dance," Jacob says nervously.

"So, what's the problem man? You're an outgoing guy. Just ask her, she won't be able to say no to that smile of yours."

"Well, she is really beautiful, and she plays volleyball. She has a game today. Actually, I intend to ask her after the game," Jacob says, feeling a little more confident.

"Like I said, you've got this, buddy," Dylan responds with a smile in his voice.

"Thanks, buddy, I needed a little boost of confidence. How are things going for you?"

"Everything is pretty good. I have a lot of homework though. It's close to the end of the semester, you know."

"Oh, okay. Better take care of that. Thanks again and I'll call to let you know how it goes, maybe later tonight."

"Sounds good, you'll do all right, talk to you later, Jacob."

Over the past weekend, Jacob has purchased a white volleyball at Dick's Sporting Goods.

He had told his mom, "You cannot just ask a girl to go to the Homecoming dance. You have to be creative."

And creative he was! In the middle of a white volleyball, he neatly printed his invitation.

LET'S 'SET' IT UP

☐ YES ☐ NO

HOMECOMING?

Jacob has thought about doing his "ask" this way for a while and hopes that this will impress Kendall enough to get her to say yes. Before leaving for school that morning, he had asked his mom if she thought that his idea was good enough.

"Sure, it's very creative. I think that she will like it, and probably agree to go with you," she had told him.

Jacob's mom is always home when he leaves for school and when he gets back home. Abecca works remotely. This is an arrangement that she had made with her boss when Jacob started middle school. She believes that young children are fine in after-school programs but as they reach their pre-teen and teenage years, they need more parental guidance. She is determined to give Jacob the supervision that she feels is necessary. She wants Jacob to be kind, polite, and caring to others. After Jacob left that morning, she thought, *how cool, my son is creative too!*

When Jacob goes back inside the gymnasium the score is tied at 2-2. He watches as the Coyotes and Tigers—both teams having good athletes—fight to win the game. In the end, the Tiger girls score the winning point. Jacob hopes that Kendall will not be too disappointed with the loss. Her team has won six games and lost four throughout the season. The Tigers have won seven games and lost three. They have four more games to play.

Kendall doesn't see Jacob, so she walks into the locker room and changes into her regular clothes. She throws her uniform, knee pads, ankle braces, and shoes into her duffle bag and starts to walk out to the gym. Just as she is about to open the door one of her teammates, Karen Wells, a little taller than Kendall, with auburn hair and braces says, "Hey Kendall good game!"

"Yeah, I guess. But even though we really played hard, we still lost."

"Well, we have four more games, and they are only one game ahead of us. We still have a good chance to be league champions."

"That's true," Kendall replies as she opens the door.

When Kendall comes out of the locker room, she sees that Jacob and the other volunteers have finished taking down the net, poles, and padding and have stored them away.

Smiling sheepishly with the volleyball behind his back, Jacob walks towards her. "Hey Kendall," he says, "sorry that your team lost."

"Yeah well, I guess it was their time," Kendall replies, trying not to show her disappointment.

As he approaches closer, Jacob produces his creative volley-ball and hands it to Kendall. She takes it, and as her face begins to turn a light shade of pink, she reads what he has written. A moment later she smiles saying, "That's really cute and yes, I would like to go to the Homecoming dance with you."

Distracted because of Jacob's creative invitation, she almost forgets to ask him if he knows EG. "Hey Jacob, do you know a girl named Eve Greene?"

"Nope, I don't. But my friend, Kyle Brown, said that he met a new girl named Eve the other day."

Jacob is so happy that he has impressed Kendall with his invitation and that she has said 'yes,' that it doesn't occur to him to ask her why she wants to know about Eve.

Kendall knows Kyle from church. The connection becomes obvious and Kendall thinks

… living in such a small town somebody always knows somebody who knows somebody else. She smiles, amused at this thought.

Kyle Brown, a tall, skinny, brown-haired boy, with grey eyes sings in the choir at Mount Zion Church. He is also the Youth Leader for Kendall's age group. Kendall has talked to Kyle a few times, but mostly she has listened to his instructions while either playing various games or practicing scriptures at their youth group on Monday nights.

Kyle isn't in the same grade as Jacob. He is a senior. He is not really looking forward to graduation as much as most people think. He is going to go to Northwestern College in Idaho. That's a long way from home for him. He is very close with his mom and does not want to be that far away from her. He hasn't told either of his parents how he feels. He does not want to disappoint them. Kyle's parents attended Northwestern College and want him to go there too. Most days he just pushes the thought of being far away from home out of his mind and gets on with his day. He is usually busy with school, track practice, and his Youth Group Leader responsibilities.

Liam has just pulled up in front of the school a few minutes before Kendall's game is over. She walks out and climbs into his car.

"Hi, Dad."

"Hi, how was your game?"

"Well, we really tried, but we lost."

"You will get 'em next game," Liam says with a vote of confidence in his voice.

On the way home Kendall is quiet. She is thinking about Eve and Kyle and she wonders if Kyle knows that Eve is taking drugs. She really doesn't think that Kyle would condone that kind of behavior. Maybe Kyle knows and is already trying to get Eve to stop taking drugs. Or maybe he has no idea; she does not think that Kyle has known Eve for very long. So how could he know?

Now Kendall knows that she must talk to Kyle and tell him what Jen has heard in Ms. Heather's office. She also needs to let Jen and Emma know that she has made progress on finding EG.

Kendall has not planned to go to Jen's house after her volleyball game. She is pretty sure that her mom will have dinner ready when she and her dad get home. Once Kendall and Liam get home, the Murphy family sit down for dinner. Tonight, Kate has prepared fried chicken, mashed potatoes and serves it with some store-bought coleslaw.

Kendall is anxious to talk to Jen and Emma too. She eats her dinner fairly quickly and asks if she can be excused. Normally, Kendall's parents like to talk and ask her about her day after dinner. But her mom says that it's okay with her if Kendall helps clean up from dinner.

Kendall takes the plates and silverware from the table and brings them into the kitchen.

"Please rinse everything and put them into the dishwasher," Kate calls out to Kendall.

"I'm on it, Mom."

Kendall scrapes the food from each plate, rinses them, and places them in the dishwasher. Then she rinses the silverware as well. She washes the sharp knives by hand, dries them, and puts them away in the drawer. She runs the garbage disposal and wipes down all the counters in the kitchen. She looks around the kitchen satisfied that she has done a good job of cleaning up.

Kendall walks through the dining room on her way to her room.

"Is the kitchen clean?"

"Yes Ma'am, it is spotless," Kendall says with a little eye roll, that luckily for her, Kate did not catch.

SEVEN

KYLE KNOWS EVE

Kendall walks into her room with her iPhone in her hand. She types a text to Jen:

"Hey, we have to talk"

Jen hears the familiar chime of her phone, picks it up, and sees a text message from Kendall.

Jen: *ok, what's up?*

Kendall: *should we add Emma?*

Jen: *no, just call me now.*

Kendall presses the info icon on her phone then the call icon.

"Hey," Jen says.

"Well, I have a lot of news! First Jacob asked me to go to the Homecoming dance and I said yes. He is so sweet and cute too. He actually spelled out his invitation on a volleyball. How cool is that?" Kendall bubbles.

"Homecoming dance, huh? Your parents are allowing you to go?" asks Jen, feeling her face blush as a hint of jealousy set in.

"I haven't asked them yet. But I think if we go as a group there should be no problem," Kendall replies with confidence. "But that's not all. I almost forgot, but then I asked Jacob if he knows EG."

Kendall is a couple of months older than Jen and since she is an only child, her parents tend to treat her differently, like she is older. They allow her to do things that Jen is not allowed to do. Things like going to a dance with a boy. Oftentimes Jen is jealous about that. *Of course, it would be no problem; your parents always let you do things that mine do not.*

Then Jen's mind snaps back to Kendall's last remark.

"I almost forgot, but I did ask Jacob if he knows EG."

Kendall had had the nerve to ask Jacob!

"Well, does Jacob know her?"

"No, he doesn't. But he said that my Youth Group Leader, Kyle Brown, does. I didn't even know that Jacob and Kyle knew each other."

Kendall has seen Jacob at church but has never seen him around Kyle. She just knows that Jacob's father is sometimes the substitute for Pastor Bryant. Once in a while, Pastor Bryant will have to go out of town and Mr. Anderson will take his place conducting the worship services.

A Pastor is the leader of a Christian congregation who also gives advice and counsel to people from the community or congregation. A Pastor could be ordained or not (even a layperson may serve in this capacity). Kendall doesn't know if Mr. Anderson is ordained or not. She just knows that his talks are very intriguing. *Intriguing*—another one of Mrs. Collins' unusual words; it means extremely interesting.

"So, what are we going to do with this information?"

"I have youth group on Monday night and I'm planning to tell Kyle what you heard in Ms. Heather's office," Kendall announces.

"Won't you see Kyle on Sunday at church?"

Jen doesn't really understand that much about religion. Her family does not attend a church like Kendall's family attends Mount Zion and Emma's family goes to Saint Bernard's Catholic Church.

It is interesting to Jen that Emma's family goes to

church—actually, it is called "Mass"—on Saturday evening, while Kendall's family attends on Sunday mornings. Over the years, Jen has gone to church with both Kendall and Emma a few times. Usually, it was for a special occasion like Easter, or one time, she went to Christmas midnight Mass with Emma's family. But she is happy to be able to sleep in, have a family big breakfast in pajamas then read the comics on most Sunday mornings.

Jen's parents had explained to her, once she was old enough to understand, that her father is Buddhist. Buddhists can worship both at home or at a temple. For Buddhists, it is not considered essential to go to a temple to worship with others. There is no belief in a personal God. Buddhists believe that nothing is fixed or permanent (no state, good or bad, lasts forever) and that change is the nature of the universe.

"I'll see him because he's in the choir, but I don't usually have a chance to talk to him. I think that I would probably have his full attention at group."

"Yeah sure, if you think that you can talk to Kyle on Monday night. But what is your plan? Are you going to just blurt out that EG is taking drugs?"

"Well, I figured that I would tell Kyle what you heard in Ms. Heather's office the other day. Just give him the whole story the way that you told me and Emma."

"Do you think that he already knows that EG is taking drugs?"

"I don't know. I don't think that he has known EG all that long."

"We need to tell Emma what your plan is too. Let's meet up at my house tomorrow morning and walk over to Emma's."

"Yeah, that sounds good. What time, like nine or nine-thirty?"

"I guess around there sounds good."

"Okay, I'll see you tomorrow, good night."

"Good night."

Kendall has forfeited watching TV so that she can talk to Jen tonight. It is almost time for bed now. She puts on her long-sleeved thermal pajamas, brushes her teeth, and picks up her book *The Book Thief*, and begins to read.

Hans sees the book that Liesel stole from the bonfire. With a wink and a smile, Hans promises not to tell Rosa, and Liesel promises to keep any secret for him if ever he asks her to. Liesel also identifies the mayor's wife, Ilsa Hermann, as the lady with fluffy hair who saw her take the book. Frau Hermann lives at 8 Grande Strausse. Liesel, considering her knowledge that Frau Hermann saw her take the book, begins to avoid the mayor's house on her rounds picking up and delivering laundry. When Liesel finally gets the courage to go to the mayor's house, Frau Hermann invites her into the library, where Liesel is amazed by the room filled with books. She spins around in awe unable to believe what her eyes are witnessing. Liesel continues to go to the mayor's house and begins reading while sitting on the floor of the library. She eventually finds a book with Johann Hermann written on the inside cover. Frau Hermann tells her that he was her son and that he died during World War One. Liesel tells Frau Hermann that she is sorry for her loss. When she is not reading or delivering laundry Liesel plays soccer with Rudy.

Kendall is sleepy now. She sets her book down, walks into the living room where her parents are watching TV, gives them each a hug and a kiss then goes back to her room to bed. She falls asleep thinking about Liesel and Rudy. *Rudy is always hungry, and Liesel is sick of pea soup. They join a gang of young-*

sters who steal apples and Liesel eats so many that she vomits. Ha, too many apples! Well, at least it's not candy giving her the stomachache ... Kendall thinks and smiles as she drifts off to sleep.

Jen has also decided to read before going to sleep. She is reading *The Grapes of Wrath*. This chapter has been devoted to the movement of a seemingly unimportant creature, a turtle. However, the old turtle trying to cross the highway can represent the Joad family and their struggles. Like the turtle, the Joads are victims of their very unfriendly environment, yet, also like the turtle, they continue their journey. The journey takes the turtle in a southwest direction, the same direction in which the Joads are traveling.

One car swerves onto the shoulder to avoid hitting the turtle. Yet, moments later, a truck purposely clips the shell of the turtle, sending it spinning off the highway and landing on its back. It takes a great amount of strength on the turtle's part to turn itself over and climb down the embankment to continue its way. A very determined turtle indeed!

Jen thinks about how determined she, Kendall, and Emma are to find Eve. She knows that it is extremely important to find Eve and save her from drugs. She starts to fall asleep then remembers that she has not brushed her teeth. She puts her book down, goes into the bathroom, brushes her teeth, then climbs back into bed, drifting off to sleep thinking about the turtle.

Morning comes faster than expected for Jen. She gets up and rushes through breakfast to meet Kendall on time.

"Hey Jen!" says Kendall as she walks up the sidewalk.

"Hey!"

The girls walk down toward Emma's house. Once there, they walk up her walkway and knock on her door.

"Hi, what's up?" Emma says, as she opens the door.

"Well, a lot happened yesterday afternoon and last night. First, you know Jacob Anderson, right?" asks Kendall.

"Sure. The boy that you showed us in the yearbook."

"He asked me to go to the Homecoming dance. He is so sweet and cute too. He actually wrote the invitation on a volleyball. How creative is that? And of course, I said yes!" Kendall repeats what Jen has already heard.

Jen tries to be patient with Kendall. *My God, this is not the reason that we are here!*

"Then I asked Jacob if he knows EG," Kendall breaks into Jen's thought.

"So, does he know her?"

"No, he doesn't. But he said that my youth group leader, Kyle, does."

"So, what are we going to do?"

"I have youth group on Monday night and I'm planning to tell Kyle what Jen heard in Ms. Heather's office. I'll tell him everything that Jen told us."

"That sounds like a really good idea."

"Well, I have to go shopping with my mom now," Jen says.

"I have a few things to do too," Kendall adds.

"Thanks for letting me know what's been going on with your plan, Kendall."

Jen and Kendall head back up the street towards their houses. Jen goes up her walkway and Kendall takes the shortcut across their adjoining lawns.

"Hey Mom, I'm back, are you ready to go shopping?" Jen calls out to her mom.

"I'll be right there," Robin responds.

Layla and Robin rush into the kitchen and Robin motions to Jen to open the door.

"Hey Jeff, the girls and I are going to the mall now!" Robin shouts as they leave.

EIGHT

LUCIA'S QUINCEAÑERA

Emma watches as Jen and Kendall walk down the sidewalk towards their houses. She and her parents are going to her cousin Lucia's Quinceañera this afternoon.

In Argentina, the ceremony is known as the "Fiesta de Quince," a celebration for a girl turning fifteen years old. The ceremony begins with the daughter making a grand entrance to a slow song, through a specially decorated door accompanied by her father.

When people think of birthdays in the United States their minds generally think of cake. While Argentinians do not serve up birthday cakes, they are definitely not short on delicious treats perfectly fit for any birthday celebration. It would not be a typical Argentine dessert if it did not involve dulce de leche (caramel) in some form or another.

Emma is looking forward to chocotorta and alfajor rogel. Chocotorta combines chocolate wafer cookies, coffee laced with Kahlua, cream cheese, and dulce de leche. Rogel is a classic dessert consisting of numerous thin layers of crispy cookie-like dough that are topped with a creamy dulce de leche spread. The cake traditionally includes eight layers, while the top is usually decorated with Italian meringue.

She also knows that there will be milanesa (pronounced mee-lah-neh-sah) which is made from chicken or beef that has been hammered thin and then rubbed with breadcrumbs before either baking or frying it. It is typically topped with a fried egg, cheese, or tomato sauce. This dish was brought to Argentina by immigrants during the Italian migration.

Argentine cuisine is a cultural blending of Mediterranean influences (such as those created by Italian and Spanish) as well as Native American influences. Argentine people have a reputation for their love of food. Sharing of food, which is traditionally homemade, is viewed as a symbol of friendship and warmth, a way to show affection.

For a Quinceañera, it is customary for friends and family to dress formally. But for Emma, the dress needs to be even more elaborate because she is a member of Lucia's close family. And much like the bridesmaids at a wedding, they are to coordinate with the birthday girl. Emma's mom, Julieta, purchased a floor-length evening gown for her that compliments Lucia's gown. It is baby blue. The fabric is satin, which has a glossy face and a matte back. It feels so soft and smooth on Emma's body. Emma has dabbed a small amount of *Daisy* behind her ears and on her neck.

Traditionally, Lucia would have worn a white ballgown like a wedding dress. In today's world, Lucia can choose from many different colors and Lucia has chosen royal blue for her gown, which features a full skirt made with layers of silk, satin, and tulle with a crinoline underneath to make the skirt flair out. Lucia will, of course, be the focal point of the event.

Emma, Julieta, and Franco get into their car to drive to Saint Bernard's Catholic Church.

"Emma, could you hold the roses for Tío Juan, please?" Franco asks.

"Sure," Emma says as she places the flowers on her lap.

Since the family is devoutly Catholic, the celebration starts with Mass to give thanks for the passing of another year. During the Mass, Lucia receives Holy Communion. She makes an act of consecration to the Virgin Mary. Consecration is the action of placing a child under the Virgin Mary's protection and asking her for her maternal blessing for them. Lucia gifts the Virgin Mary with a bouquet of flowers. In turn, Lucia receives gifts, usually a ring, a tiara, or a necklace blessed by Father Cosgrove, the priest. Tonight, he gently places a tiara on her hair.

Once the Mass is complete, Emma, Julieta, and Franco walk inside the ballroom with the other guests and wait for Lucia and Juan to enter. A slow song is playing as they come through the door that has been decorated with beautiful flowers. Franco, Julieta, and Emma share in handing Juan roses.

After this, the ceremony of the waltz begins, during which Lucia first dances with Juan who passes her on to Franco, and he, in turn, passes her on to another relative. They have selected "Tiempo De Vals" by Chayanne for this dance, a flowing ceremonial melody.

Emma is happy to see her cousin so happy. She is beautiful in her gown and her smile could not be bigger. Her thick curly hair is half up and half down with what is called a 'basket weave' in the back. Baby's breath has been woven elegantly into her hair so that she appears to be a princess.

Once Lucia has waltzed with each of her relatives and friends, it is time for the entrée, or appetizer. Emma finds one of her favorite foods—asado which consists of beef, pork, and chicken cooked on a grill with red-hot coals and firewood. A simple iron grill called a parrilla is used. Emma breathes in the smell of the meat mixed with the maple firewood; she is hungry. She spots the empanadas, baked dough stuffed with chicken or beef; Emma chooses to take one of each. She takes a small amount of salad too.

The celebration moves on to dancing to international music. The music is loud, and the party gets louder as well. "El Rey y Su Cadillac" by Paulo Franco and the Freightliners is playing and Emma is having a great time bouncing to the beat with her cousins. Franco and Julieta dance as well. With so much going on, Juan, Franco's brother, has very little time to talk. He is rushing around greeting all the guests.

"This is such a great party!" Franco calls out as Juan passes by while he and Julieta dance.

As the evening goes on, it is time for the main course meal. Emma, Julieta, and Franco find their table and sit down. Much like a wedding reception, each table is called to go through the buffet line. Emma has been patiently waiting for milanesa.

After the main course is served, it is time for more dancing followed by dessert. "I want chocotorta and alfajor rogel!" Emma shouts over the music to Julieta.

"Don't eat too many sweets, you'll likely end up with the stomachache," Franco warns Emma.

"Please let her have fun," Julieta says softly as she leans into Franco's ear.

After all the waltzing, eating, and dancing, the "Tree of Life" ceremony begins. Here, Lucia delivers one lit candle to each of the fifteen most influential people in her life. She gives a heartwarming speech as she individually acknowledges how each recipient has impacted her life. The fifteen candles symbolize the fifteen years that she has left behind.

First is her father, Juan. "Papi, you have always been here for me. You've attended soccer and softball games, plays, and other musical events that I have participated in. Thank you, I love you!" Lucia says as she hands her first candle to her dad.

Next is her mother, Carmen's turn. "Mama, you have cared for me. You've cooked my food and sewn my clothes. You are always here when I am happy and when I am sad or sick. Thank you for being my momma," Lucia said with tears in her eyes as she hands the lit candle to her mom.

Then it is Franco's turn. "Tío, you have been such a huge part of my life. You are always here to give me advice and you usually come to my soccer games. Thank you so much," Lucia says as she hands the third candle to Franco.

The next candle is for Julieta. "Nina, you are a huge part of my life too. You've given me the best gift ever, Emma! Thank you for coming tonight and for always taking me and Emma to the movies and shopping too," Lucia tells Julieta as she places the fourth candle in her hand.

Now it is Emma's turn. "Emma, you are one of my cousins, but more than that you are my first friend. My best friend! We can talk about anything and everything together. We laugh and sing and have such fun. Thank you for always being my best friend!" Lucia smiles from ear to ear while tears well up in her eyes as she hands Emma the fifth candle.

Lucia continues the ritual of handing the candles to each of the people who have shared a memory or special moment with her until all fifteen have been handed out.

The third period of dancing is followed by everyone honoring Lucia.

Juan proudly stands with his arm around Carmen's shoulders, speaking into the crowd. "Let's raise our glasses to offer a toast to Lucia. May God bless you today and every day after! We give thanks to God for all that Lucia brings to our lives, so much happiness and laughter. Feliz cumpleaños, mi amor!"

Lastly, there is the ribbon ritual; each female relative and friend pulls a ribbon out of a bunch. The ribbons all have charms on the ends except for one which has a ring, it symbolizes the circle of life and the importance of cycles.

Once the celebration is gradually ending, Emma, Julieta, and Franco say their goodbyes to Lucia, Carmen, and Juan.

"Lucia, I had a blast. I ate. I danced. And I ate some more. This was such a fun night!" Emma bubbles.

"It was so much fun having you here tonight!" Lucia, still sparkling head to toe, replies with a gorgeous smile. Then she kisses Emma on her cheek and hugs her tightly.

"Carmen, you look so beautiful even after all the work of putting on such a wonderful party," Julieta says.

"It was great to have you come tonight. It won't be long before you will be planning Emma's Quinceañera, Julie," Carmen replies as she hugs Julieta.

"You sure did a great job on this party Juan," Franco congratulates his brother.

"Thank you. Soon it will be your turn for your beautiful, Emma," Juan replies as he slaps Franco on the back.

The Perez family walks out into the cool night air and climbs into their car. On the way home, Emma, having danced and eaten so much, feels exhausted, and as she gets comfy in the backseat of the Perezmobile, it's as if her full petticoat and dress is ready to collapse as well. She drifts off to sleep to the gentleness of the car's humming tires. It's late so there is not much traffic.

Emma dreams of how difficult it was for Scout to learn, the hard way, that she was different from all the other students in her class. Much to Scout's teacher's surprise, Scout had entered the first grade already knowing how to read and write. *Doesn't everyone already know how to read and write?*

Emma then finds herself back at the party. She's dancing and spots Scout sitting at one of the grand tables in her scruffy t-shirt and sneakers, scribbling madly with her nose in her notebook. She also notices over in the corner a girl who looks to be high on drugs and Emma begins to feel like a hive of bees is buzzing in her stomach ... .

NINE

A MYSTERIOUS MEETING

Jen knows that Emma has a lot of issues with Jimmy. She worries about him being in jail. She wonders if he might get out early for good behavior. And if he does, will their relationship be the same brother-sister relationship that it has been when he gets out?

Jen also knows that Emma does not want anyone else to suffer the way that she has. They have to solve the problem quickly and she hopes that Kendall's conversation with Kyle tonight will fix it before it gets too bad.

The way Ms. Heather is involved in all this confuses Jen. It troubles her even more than it seems to bother Kendall. All Emma has said is that she doesn't think that it is a good idea to talk to Ms. Heather about EG, but she really doesn't seem to wonder why Ms. Heather is involved, at least she hasn't mentioned it.

The Columbia School District has a section for preschool children. Today Jen's elective class is to help in the library of the preschool. She shakes the thoughts about Ms. Heather out of her mind as she opens the door to the preschool building. She wants to be sure that she is happy for the children and doesn't want to seem distracted. She waves hello to the person at the front desk and walks back into the activities room. The Director is setting the room up. She usually sits in a large armchair with small chairs for the kids in a half-circle in front of it.

Mrs. Lenhart greets Jen when she sees her walk in. "How are you doing today?"

Most people will ask that question as a greeting, they don't really expect an in-depth answer, and they usually expect a simple "fine" in response. However, Jen has long ago learned that when it comes to Mrs. Lenhart, she wants an honest answer.

When Mrs. Lenhart asks anyone how they are doing, she stops what she is doing, focuses on the person, and waits for their answer. Jen has learned not to give Mrs. Lenhart a quick or incomplete answer.

"It's a beautiful day, my classes are going well, so I'm really good."

"That's great," Mrs. Lenhart replies with a smile before shifting her attention back to arranging the room. Jen begins pulling out more folding chairs from the closet when she hears Mrs. Lenhart snap her fingers.

"Jen! I almost forgot."

"What did you forget, Mrs. Lenhart?"

"I'm reading *Beezus and Ramona* to the children today, but the book is pretty short even for this bunch. I want another Ramona book, but we do not have any more here. I called over to the main building and Mr. Lewis said that he has a copy of *Ramona the Brave*. Could you go over and get it for me, please?"

"Of course, I will."

After all, that is the reason she is there; it is her responsibility to help in any way that Mrs. Lenhart requests. She knows it is a short walk over to the main building; it will only take two or three minutes.

The Ramona series is composed from the older sister Beezus' point of view. In the first book, *Beezus and Ramona*, Beezus battles with affections for her somewhat irritating younger sister. In the end, Beezus acknowledges that it is possible to love her sister, notwithstanding when she does not generally like her.

Jen finishes unfolding the chair she has in her hands.

"I'll be right back."

She heads out the back door, which takes her out near the parking lot of the school. As she is walking towards the front of the school, she sees a woman, wearing an elegant navy-blue pantsuit, stepping out of an SUV that looks like an Escalade. She has medium-length auburn, curly hair and is carrying a black briefcase. Jen spots the car magnet on the driver's side door which reads White Realty. This is Derek's mother, which is strange. Why would she be at school in the middle of the day?

With Jen's curiosity piqued, she slows her pace a bit and lets the woman walk past her. There is a look of determination on the woman's face and in her walk; she is obviously on a mission of some sort. She does not hold the door for Jen, even though she is only about five or six feet behind her. As Jen opens the door and enters the building, Derek's mother turns toward the opposite hallway that Jen needs to go. But the halls all end up going in one large square, so Jen follows her, knowing that she will be able to see where Derek's mother is going and pick up *Ramona the Brave* from Mr. Lewis too. Jen allows

Derek's mother to get about twenty feet ahead of her, that way she can see her and not be noticeable.

Derek's mother walks around one corner, and the next, and eventually turns into a set of doors that Jen knows to be the guidance counselor's office. When Jen walks by, she sees Derek in the office with his mother, along with Mrs. Collins and the guidance counselor. She hears the door shut with a clunk and thinks—*Well, that is the end of that.* She is not going to be able to find out why Derek and his mother are there without listening at the door, so she continues around the square until she arrives at Mr. Lewis' room. She gets the book and heads back through the main entrance to the activities room. All the while her mind races with the question *what is Mrs. White doing here?* Jen knows that Derek had disrupted class the other day. But is that serious enough for a meeting with the teacher and guidance counselor? After all, he wasn't late to class and he did hand his iPod over to Mrs. Collins without an incident. So, what is the big deal anyway?

After school Jen, Emma and Kendall head to Layla's school to pick her up, and as the four continue to their neighborhood, Jen says, "I saw Derek White, his mother, and Mrs. Collins in the guidance counselor's office today. I don't know what's going on, but I don't think that his iPod incident was that earth-shaking, do you?"

"No, I don't think so," Emma replies.

"Me neither," Kendall says.

"Well, I wonder why she would've had to meet with Mrs. Collins," Jen challenges.

"Who knows, maybe there's something else going on with Derek that we don't know about," Emma offers.

Since Kendall has her youth group meeting tonight and

they have nothing much to talk about, they have not planned to study together today.

"I'll see you tomorrow," Emma says as they approach her house.

"Yeah, see you tomorrow," Jen replies as she, Kendall, and Layla continue towards their homes.

"Well, good luck talking to Kyle tonight," Jen tells Kendall as she cuts across their adjoining lawns.

"I'm a little nervous but we have to find EG and help her."

"Yeah, this is *so* important. You know?

Once in their house, Jen immediately says, "Layla let's get started on our homework," as she sits herself down at the dining room table. She motions to Layla to sit with her and Layla dutifully obeys. If they finish early, they might have time to watch a sitcom before their mom and dad get home.

TEN

PROVERBS AND FRIENDSHIP

Kendall's mom has made pork chops, fried potatoes, coleslaw, and apple sauce for dinner tonight. As the Murphy family sits down in the dining room to eat, Kendall tries to avoid any deep conversation because her focus is on talking to Kyle.

"So, you have youth group tonight, right?" her mother asks.

"Yes, Mrs. S will be here soon."

Mrs. Strickland, otherwise known as Mrs. S, is the mother of Amy Strickland, another girl that Kendall knows from youth group. She gives Kendall a ride each week because Kendall's house is on her way to the church.

After dinner, Kendall takes her plate and silverware to the kitchen and puts them on the counter. Then she walks toward the front door. When she is halfway out the door she calls back, "I'll see you later, Mom and Dad."

"Hi Mrs. S how are you?" asks Kendall as she gets into the car and smiles at Amy.

"I'm doing very well, Kendall, how are you?"

"Oh, I'm good. School is going good."

"Well let's get you both off to Group then," Mrs. S says,

shifting her car into drive. She looks quickly for any oncoming traffic and pulls away from the curb onto the street.

The drive is a short three and a half miles to the church. Once there, Kendall looks for Kyle, though she does not see him right away. A few of the other teens are walking into the meeting room. Amy is slightly ahead of Kendall.

"Hey Kendall, how's it going?" Mike asks as he walks in.

"Hi Mike, I'm good."

"Hey, what's up, Kendall?" Ricky asks as he follows Mike in.

"I'm doing okay, how about you?"

"Everything is going all right, I guess."

Mike is a tall, skinny, brown-eyed boy with black hair, and Ricky Duran is his twin brother. They live in the next town over, Greenville, which is about a 20-minute drive. Kendall only sees them at their youth group or other church-related events. Even though they are identical twins, Kendall thinks that Ricky is the cuter of the two. That is probably because he is the most outgoing. Mike is shy, and he does not say very much to anyone. Of course, since they do not attend her school, they would not know anything about the EG situation. Yet, at the same time, Kendall does not want to talk to Kyle in front of them. She is beginning to wonder if talking about EG would be gossiping. After all, Proverbs 20:19 states, "Whoever goes about slandering reveals secrets; therefore, do not associate with a simple babbler."

But when you are trying to help someone, is it really gossiping? she wonders.

Just as she's lost in thought, Kyle walks into the room. "Hey, guys, how's everybody doing?"

In turn, each person in the group nods hello or reports that they are doing fine and all are ready to play some games in the church's gym. Tonight, they will be playing kickball.

In this game, there is a person who, much like a pitcher in baseball, rolls a large rubber ball to a team member situated at home plate, and the one "up to bat," so-to-speak, kicks it and runs to first base. If the ball is not caught right away, the kicker runs to the next base. Another team member comes to home plate and the process is repeated.

The group gets up from the chairs and begins to walk over to the next building where the gym is located.

Kyle hands out wrist bands; actually, they are hair scrunchies, red to one team and blue to the other. Ricky ends up on the red team with Kendall, and Mike is on the blue team.

When Kyle hands the red scrunchie to Kendall, she asks, "Could we talk, in private, later?"

"Um sure, I guess," Kyle answers. "What's up?"

Kendall cautiously replies, "It's kind of a private thing that I need to ask you about."

"Well, okay. We can talk after the kickball game, all right?"

Kendall gives Kyle a shy smile. "That'll work for me."

The blue team is up first. Kenny Rose, a lanky, brown-haired boy with green eyes kicks the ball over the heads of everyone on the red team. He runs to first base and then to second as Ricky struggles to get control of the ball. Ricky throws the ball to their second base team member, Cathy Long, but she retrieves the ball too late and Kenny is already safe on second base.

Kendall is the third base team member. She needs to be aware that Kenny is going to be running towards her as soon as Charlie kicks the ball.

Charlie is Cathy's brother; he is wearing jeans that are too big and droop down. *Those pants should make it hard for him to run,* Kendall thinks as she watches the ball rolling towards

Charlie. She then turns her attention to Kenny. Charlie kicks the ball to Rob Gordon, the pitcher, who catches it and throws it to Kendall; she taps Kenny with the ball when he runs toward her. Two outs!

Back and forth the teams play, scoring almost evenly. They laugh, shout, and tease each other in good will as each team member kicks the ball while other members try and catch it. In the end, the red team wins the game by a score of six to five. The kids wrap up the game, putting the ball and bases away in the gym's storage room.

Kyle gathers everyone and says, "Let's go back to study the scriptures," so the group walks back from the gym toward the meeting room in the main church building. Kendall taps Kyle on the shoulder and asks, "Is now a good time to talk?"

"Sure."

The other teens, who have worked up an appetite for the snacks and drinks on the table, go into the room and take their seats, while Kyle and Kendall remain behind in the hall.

"So, what's up?" Kyle breaks the ice.

"Well," Kendall says, looking him in the eye, "I talked to Jacob Anderson the other day. He actually asked me to go to the Homecoming dance—but that's not what I want to talk to you about. He said that you know a girl named Eve Greene." Kendall holds her breath, wondering if Kyle will offer some identification for High Girl.

"Yes, I recently met Eve. Why do you want to know?"

"Well, my friend, Jen, was sick the other day so she was in Ms. Heather's office."

"What does that have to do with Eve?"

"Jen fell asleep and when she woke up, she heard someone, a girl, telling Ms. Heather that she was high and had been all morning."

"I still don't see how this involves Eve."

"I—well, I mean my friends, Jen and Emma, did some research. Jen actually saw that the last name written on Ms. Heather's check-in form was Greene."

"You guys did research? How?"

"At first we didn't know where to start. We looked at past yearbooks, looking for anyone with the name Greene. But we didn't have any luck there."

"So how do you know her name is Eve?"

"Well, we did a search on Google for people named Greene. But that didn't work either. All we got was a lot of pretty much trivial information about actors and other celebrities. But, then Jen's little sister, Layla, who's only in 3rd grade, overheard us talking and she said that she knew a girl named Connie Greene who recently moved here."

"Well, that's still not Eve Greene."

"No, but we asked Layla to ask Connie if she has a sister at our school. She does and her name is Eve."

"Okay, we really need to get back into the meeting room and go over the scriptures. Speaking of which—you do know that this is considered 'gossip'—" Kyle adds. "But we can talk more about this after we study."

By this time, the group is settling down and waiting patiently for Kyle and Kendall to come into the room. Kyle takes his place at the head of the table, announcing, "Let's get started," as he sits down. He begins with "Life is tough. Just because we have a relationship with God, we cannot assume that life on earth is going to be a breeze. In fact, the Bible tells us repeatedly that we will surely encounter suffering, and the Bible encourages us to persevere through it."

Kyle clears his throat and continues, "As we make our way through this life, we will encounter hard days, trials, suffering, and obstacles. And we cannot do it alone. That's the reason the Bible talks about the importance of true friendship."

Pausing to take a sip of his water, he continues, "Let's read Ecclesiastes chapter four verses nine through ten: *Two are better than one, because they have a good reward for their toil. For if they fall, one will lift up his fellow. But woe to him who is alone when he falls and has not another to lift him up.*"

Kyle sits for a moment to let the reading sink in, then says, "Verse ten tells us that having a friend is important because when we are working hard toward a goal, we have someone to help us through it. We all want someone to feel the same way as we do, someone to be on our side and get it, right?"

"Now, let's read Proverbs chapter twenty-seven verse seventeen ... " Kyle takes another sip of water before he begins to read: "*Iron sharpens iron, and one man sharpens another.* Who has an idea of what this means?"

Cathy raises her hand and answers, "I think it has to do with being accountable."

"Very good, Cathy, we sometimes don't want to talk about accountability. Part of any valuable friendship is the ability to be open and honest with one another," Kyle replies.

"So, *The Book of Proverbs, 27:5*, reminds us that even though it might be challenging to hear the truth from a friend, if we are willing to have an open mind and open heart, we will grow from it," Kyle goes on, "Evaluate your friendships."

"Let's take these questions home with us and think about them. (1) Do you find it hard to hold friends accountable?

Why or why not? (2) Do you fear ending friendships that are not good for you? (3) Are there any aspects of your friendships that you want to change? We can talk about your answers next week," Kyle finishes, hoping he has provoked the group to think the questions over.

As the other teens file out of the room, Kyle asks Kendall to hang back. "I want to think about what you have told me and to talk to Eve. I'll get back to you in a day or so—once I have a chance to figure this out."

"Okay. But Emma is really worried about Eve because as you know her brother Jimmy and his situation ... " Kendall trails off.

Kyle had heard one of Emma's talks about Jimmy in the auditorium last year when Jimmy was arrested. He knows the trouble that Jimmy has caused the Perez family. This concerns him. But he does not know Eve well enough to either suspect her of taking drugs, or not. Now Kyle needs to talk to Eve and try to figure this whole thing out before rumors, whether true or false, begin to spin out of control.

Once out of the building, Kendall lowers her head to avoid a cold wind which has swept up the dry grass. Suddenly she notices an ant hill with dozens of the little bugs scampering around, up, down, and over each other, as if all abuzz with important news or a juicy piece of gossip. Kendall can't help but think of how gossip can spread, how everyone had heard about Emma's brother Jimmy as soon as it happened. After staring at the confusion for a few minutes, she pulls her jacket tighter, spots Amy, and heads toward her.

ELEVEN

TRUTHS REVEALED

Kyle is thinking about the talks Emma gave in the auditorium last year about her brother, Jimmy. He knows how much pain Jimmy has caused Emma and her family. He does not know Eve very well, yet he feels he needs to talk to her about taking drugs. Kyle is certain he must talk to Eve; he does not want any rumors to get out of hand.

What does the Bible say about rumors? Kyle thinks to himself and recalls *James 3:5 Likewise, the tongue is a small part of the body, but it makes great boasts. Consider what a great forest is set on fire by a small spark.*

"Well, we certainly do not need a forest fire!" he says to himself.

Kyle decides to talk to his mom about this situation. His mom will be able to give him good advice on what to do next. He has always been able to count on her.

ↄ৲

Tammy Brown is a stay-at-home mother. She decided a long time ago that she would choose Home Economist for her career. She went to Northwestern College and studied business administration, which helped her with juggling the family's budget in the early years of their marriage.

The Browns, Tammy, and Jim, have three children. Kyle is the eldest, Owen is the middle child and Logan is their youngest. Owen is a freshman in high school and Logan is in 6th grade. The two younger boys love baseball and football as does their father. Sometimes Tim takes the boys to professional games. Tim also likes to play golf and often takes Owen with him. Tammy and Tim both like music. One of their favorite singers is Lauren Daigle, who is compared to the heart-in-throat vulnerability of Adele mixed with the raw power of Amy Winehouse. Her Grammy-winning single, "*You Say*" has appeared in the Top 40 of Billboard's Hot 100 Chart. Tammy is hoping that she and Tim will be able to attend Lauren's upcoming concert at the Extra Mile Arena in Boise. She wants to take Kyle too since he loves singing.

Just as she's daydreaming about the concert, Kyle comes into the room.

"Mom, I have a situation that I need to talk to you about," Kyle states, tossing his backpack on a chair and sliding himself into another chair at the kitchen table.

"What kind of a situation?" Tammy asks anxiously.

"Well, do you know Kendall Murphy?"

"No, I don't think that I know who she is."

"She is in my youth group."

"Is she in some sort of trouble?"

"Well, no, I don't think so. But she told me something disturbing tonight."

"So, this is something about another person?"

"Yes. Do you remember that I told you about the new girl that I met a couple of weeks ago—Eve?"

"Yes, but now I'm a little confused. How is Kendall connected to Eve?"

"Well, I don't know Eve well enough to know if this is a rumor or not. But tonight, Kendall said that she is concerned about Eve."

"Why?"

"It's sort of a long story, but, let me try to explain," Kyle begins and then continues to relay Kendall's story of Jen's visit to the nurse's office, how the High Girl came in and how Jen had seen the chart with the name 'Greene.'

"Ms. Heather told the girl to check back with her in an hour because she is dealing with a powerful drug. Then she left Ms. Heather's office. Jen told Kendall and their mutual friend Emma Perez, the girl whose brother Jimmy went to jail last summer for driving while on drugs. Of course, Emma got upset and wanted to find this girl. So, the three did some research; they looked at yearbooks, checked on Google and then Jen's little sister, Layla overheard them talking and said that she knows Connie Greene."

"Wow, that's a lot of information to take in, Kyle."

"I know, but we aren't to the point where I got involved—yet. They had Layla ask Connie if she has a sister at Columbia High and if she did, what was her name. Layla talked to Connie, who told her that her sister's name is Eve. Then Kendall asked Jacob Anderson if he knows Eve. And, oh yeah—also—he asked Kendall to go to the homecoming dance and she said yes, but that's another story ... "

"Okay, continue, I'm sure that you're almost there, right?" Kyle's mother says, looking intently at him.

"Right, so Jacob told Kendall that I know Eve. Then tonight between the game in the gym and scripture study,

Kendall told me this whole story. Now I don't know what to do next."

Tammy sits with Kyle for a few minutes trying to absorb all that he has told her to figure out what the best solution to the situation will be.

"We should take this slowly," she begins. "You don't know Eve very well. I think that you should give her the benefit of the doubt. You should talk to her first. You need to get her side of the story," Tammy says thoughtfully.

"Okay, that's what I was thinking too. I'll call Eve and talk to her."

"It's pretty late, Kyle, you should get some sleep. Why not talk to her in the morning?"

"Okay, Mom, thank you for helping me to sort this thing out. I can always count on you. Good night, love you!" Kyle kisses her on the cheek and goes to his room.

❧

The next morning, Kyle finds Eve at her locker in school and asks if they could have lunch together. Eve looks surprised but agrees.

Later in the day Eve and Kyle meet in the cafeteria; they both go through the line and pick out what they want. Kyle has a corn dog baked in a whole grain batter with French fries and Eve opts for the turkey sandwich with carrot sticks, grapes, and a carton of low-fat milk. They find a table over in the corner, away from the other students.

"Eve, this is going to be kind of awkward," Kyle starts the conversation.

"Well, that's a weird way to start a lunch date," Eve says with a smile trying to make light of what seems like a strange moment.

"I have something serious to ask you. And it's really hard," Kyle goes on a bit nervously.

"Okay, I know that we don't know each other that well, but you can ask me anything."

Kyle takes a deep breath and blurts out, "Do you use drugs?"

"What? No! Well, I mean not illegal drugs. I am a diabetic and I need to use insulin. I have Type 1 diabetes, which means that my body does not produce insulin. Wait, why did you even ask me that anyways?" Eve says quickly, all in one breath.

With a deep sigh of relief, Kyle says "This is going to be a very long story. So, it could take a while but don't worry, you've already clarified something."

Eve shoots him a quizzical look. "Should we meet after school to talk about this?"

"Yes, that's a good idea. We can meet in front of the school."

They finish their lunches, mostly in silence, and go to their next classes. Kyle goes to Mrs. Garcia's Spanish class and Eve heads to Mr. Monroe's History class.

Once school lets out Kyle and Eve meet and walk to Robinson Park which is a couple of streets over. They find a bench and sit down, half watching the little children playing on the swings and jungle gym.

Kyle begins, "A girl in my youth group named Kendall told me that her friend, Jen, was sick last week and went to Ms. Heather's office. She fell asleep and when she woke up, she heard Ms. Heather talking to a girl. Actually, it was you. You said that you were high and had been all day."

"That sounds right; I remember that my blood sugar was really high all day last Tuesday or was it Wednesday? Anyway, I had to go to Ms. Heather's office and check in with her,"

"What was weird to Jen is that Ms. Heather told you to

check back with her in an hour because you are dealing with a powerful drug."

"Well yes, Insulin is a powerful drug; it keeps me alive."

"Jen and Kendall have a friend, Emma, whose brother, Jimmy, used illegal drugs and had a car accident. He ended up in jail and it's been very hard for her and their family. So, when Jen told her, Emma was pretty upset."

"But I'm not taking illegal drugs," Eve states emphatically.

"I know that, but it seemed to them—from what Jen overheard—that you were. Of course, that's the problem with hearing only bits and pieces of information."

"Well, you have to tell them that I'm not doing anything wrong!"

"I think that you should have a chance to defend yourself, don't you?"

"Yes, I guess. But I don't know any of those girls and they sure don't know me."

"That's okay; I'll set something up so that we can all talk this out. Agree?"

"Agree," Eve replies feeling a bit offensive towards Jen, Kendall, and Emma.

Kyle and Eve leave the park and head back to the school where Kyle has parked his car. "Do you need a ride home, Eve?"

"No, I can call my mom and she'll come to pick me up. I have already texted her that we were going to meet up and talk after school, so she knows that I'll be late."

Kyle leaves Eve in front of the school and walks to the student parking lot. As he drives home, he remembers a quote by Gemma Troy that he had read in his Poetry class: *Remember your words can plant gardens or burn whole forests down.*

Eve waits for her mom, Deanna, for just about 10 minutes.

Deanna is a work-from-home mom. It gives her the freedom to drop the girls off at school and pick them up each day. She can attend their daytime school activities as well.

"Hi Mom," she says as she gets into the front seat of the car. Connie is already in the back passenger seat.

"How was your day, Evie?" Deanna asks.

"It was okay. Although it got a little weird after school; Kyle and I walked over to Robinson Park to talk."

"What was that all about?"

"Well, three girls think that I'm abusing drugs," Eve says with a heavy sigh. "One of them, Kendall, is in Kyle's youth group at church. She was the one who told Kyle that her friend, Jen heard me talking to Ms. Heather last week when my glucose level was too high all day. She heard me say I was 'high,' and thought that I was taking illegal drugs," Eve says as her face blushes with anger.

"Well, I hope that your new friend Kyle is going to straighten them out."

"Actually, we are all going to get together and talk. Kyle is going to set something up; probably for tomorrow after school if that's okay with you. He's a really nice guy and heads up the spiritual studies at his church."

"That will work because I have to meet with Connie's teacher after school tomorrow," Deanna replies placing her hand on Eve's shoulder noticing that she is tense. Eve stares out the window trying to figure out her immediate emotions considering this would-be scandal. Whatever they are, she knows they don't feel good.

THE RENDEZVOUS

Kyle thinks that it is a good idea to ask Kendall, Jen, and Emma to meet him and Eve at the park as it seems that this conversation cannot be finished during their lunch break, or for that matter, in school. Kyle decides to call Kendall and then have her invite Jen and Emma.

"Kendall, it's Kyle. I have some information about Eve. I would like to talk to you and your friends. Could all of you meet me at Robinson Park tomorrow after school?"

"Sure, I think so. Let me talk to them. I was just about to go over to Jen's to study. I'll ask them and call you later."

"Okay, that sounds good. Talk to you later then."

"Okay, bye."

Kendall slides her phone into her pocket, walks out the door, and cuts across the lawn to Jen's house. Without knocking, she opens the door and lets herself in.

Finding Jen and Emma in the dining room, Kendall begins, "So last night I told my Youth Group Leader, Kyle, what you heard in Ms. Heather's office."

"What did he say about this Eve person?" Emma asks.

"He said that he had to talk to Eve and that he would let me know what he finds out."

"When will that be?" Jen asks.

"Well, just before I walked out the door Kyle called and told me that he has information about Eve and he wants all of us to meet him tomorrow after school at Robinson Park."

Both Emma and Jen are anxious to meet Kyle and hear what he will have to say about Eve and her drug problem.

"I don't see why that won't work," Emma says.

"Yeah, it sounds okay to me too," Jen replies.

The rest of the afternoon and evening go pretty much as usual, studying, eating dinner, cleaning up, reading, and getting ready for bed.

In the morning Kendall, Emma, Jen, and Layla meet up to walk to school together. Nobody has much to say as they are all wondering what Kyle will say to them that afternoon.

The day is like any other school day with classes, lunchtime, and free period, until Mr. Jackson makes an announcement.

"I'm sure that everybody has noticed that Derek White has been missing for the past couple of days. I want to let you know, before any rumors get started, that Derek's dad has been hospitalized. He apparently took too much of a prescribed medication."

After school Kendall, Emma, and Jen walk to Layla's school to pick her up.

"So, I guess we know why Derek was in the counselor's office the other day," Jen says.

"Yep, that mystery is solved," Emma adds.

"Next, we'll find out what Kyle has to say about Eve," Kendall replies.

When they get close to the park, they can see that Kyle is already there sitting on a bench with a girl. Jen doesn't say anything but notices that the girl has a black backpack with orange piping on it. Of course, it has to be her.

Once they get to the bench, Kendall says as she points to each girl, "Kyle, this is Emma, Jen, and her little sister Layla."

Kyle and Eve stand to face the foursome. Eve is the same height as Jen, wearing the black Converse, jeans, and a navy-blue three-quarter-length sleeve shirt. The words, "Shine Bright," adorn the front in gold lettering. She has shoulder-length brown curly hair with light blue barrettes on either side to hold her curls back from her face.

"Ladies, this is Eve," Kyle states matter-of-factly.

There is a prolonged silence as the girls all look each other up and down and then Jen, Emma and Kendall look back at each other.

Kyle breaks the silence, "Let me start by saying that it would probably be best if Layla goes and plays on the swings."

"Yes, that's a good idea, you can go over there and play Layla," Jen replies motioning to Layla.

Layla hesitates for a moment then thinks that this is quite different from their usual afternoons of homework and takes advantage of the opportunity to play. She sees other children around her age on the swings and walks toward them.

Once Layla has left the group, Kyle starts the discussion with, "First, I want you all to know that Eve has done nothing wrong," while he looks directly at Jen, Kendall, and Emma.

Jen jumps in with, "But I heard her tell Ms. Heather that she was high! I know what I heard."

Eve shouts, "Well, you don't even know anything about me! Besides, I am standing right here, don't talk about me as if I'm not!" The girls all see her bright green eyes are half-closed into menacing slits and her voice sounds bitter.

"Sorry," Jen murmurs just a little louder than a whisper. She does not know Kyle, but she thinks that she can trust him because she knows that Kendall trusts him. Yet she knows she will have to be convinced to fully believe that she has been so wrong for these past days.

Kyle, once again looking at the girls, asks, "It's just you three who have talked about Eve and her possible drug use, right?"

They all shake their heads in acknowledgment that the rumor has not gone beyond them, which Kyle is relieved to hear. Now Kyle can dismiss the thought of a forest fire erupting and engulfing the school.

"I understand that you think that you know what you heard, Jen," Kyle offers. "But you don't really know the whole story. Eve, do you want to explain what was going on in Ms. Heather's office the other day?" Kyle asks. "You can give as much or as little information as you feel comfortable with."

Eve gives a heavy sigh. Jen notices her eyes look a little more forgiving. "I was high all day that day, but not the way that you think," she says. "I do use a powerful drug, but there is nothing illegal about it. I have to do tests every day, but not drug tests." She takes another deep breath. "I've gotten some stares before, and some people have looked at me a little funny, but I've never been accused of abusing drugs." She raises her voice, and her eyes are moistening now. Kyle puts his hand on Eve's shoulder to give her support.

Emma says, "But Jen heard you say that you were high, we thought that was a sign."

"Well, you might have thought that you saw a sign, but that's completely different from what you think you know." On the verge of tears, Eve pauses before she looks up towards the sky as if she is trying to find the right way to say something.

"You see, it's simple really. I am a diabetic. That means that my blood glucose, that is my sugar level—can get too high, which makes me feel horrible. I need to use a glucometer to test my levels; I prick my fingertip to get a small amount of blood with something called a lancet and my readings had been high all that day. I need to take insulin to keep me alive. And I have this."

Eve lifts her shirt, puts her hand in her pocket, and pulls out a little device. She holds it up. It is about the size of a deck of cards, pink and silver with a square screen on one edge, three buttons under the screen, and at the top edge, what looks like a tube coming out leads to a patch attached to Eve's stomach.

"I have this to give me the insulin."

"What is that?" Emma asks.

"This is an insulin pump. It pumps my 'powerful drug' into my body 24/7. And whenever I eat, I take this out, punch in a few numbers and take a bolus."

"What is a bolus?" Jen asks.

"So, a bolus is a single, large dose of medicine that's taken to handle a rise in my blood glucose. Basal insulin is what I need to keep my blood glucose levels in balance all day and night."

"Well," Emma says, "Now I feel really stupid."

"So do I," says Jen, as she watches Eve slip her insulin pump back into her pocket.

Kyle says, "I understand that you are nervous when it comes to drugs, Emma."

Emma looks at Eve and begins, "My brother, Jimmy was high on drugs and he attempted to rob a convenience store. He was restricted to our house all last summer, except to go to work. Our mother had to drive him because he was arrested while driving and had his license taken away. When he went to court, he agreed to plead guilty to DUI; that's 'Driving Under the Influence,' in case you don't know. And he is in jail now.

When I heard that someone was high in school, I didn't think that there was any other explanation."

Emma bites her lip to try to hold back her tears, but they come anyway. "I'm so sorry," she says, her voice breaking as tears run down her cheeks.

"It's all my fault!" Jen jumps in. "I heard you say 'high' and I totally thought that you were using drugs. I'm sorry, I am so sorry! I just wanted to help you."

"Well, I don't usually like to talk about it because it makes me different. All I want is to fit in, to be like everybody else," Eve says looking down at the ground.

Eve looks at Emma and says, "I'm sorry about your brother and I understand that you thought that you were going to help me. But you should have talked to me. All of this didn't help anyone."

"I know that now," Emma says wiping her eyes just as Layla runs up to the group.

"What's wrong with Emma?" Layla asks Jen.

"She's okay, it's nothing really, Layla." Then looking at the other girls she says, "We need to get home, it's getting late. So sorry, Eve."

"I'm happy that we could meet like this and get the situation straightened out," Kyle says like a true mediator. "Do any of you have any other questions?"

"I don't think so," Jen says.

Everyone else shakes their heads indicating that they do not.

ↄ

Emma, Kendall, Jen, and Layla walk in silence to their neighborhood. As they approach Emma's house, Kendall says, "That was close, you know that we could have been considered gossips."

Jen replies, "I guess we are gossips. I heard something, jumped to a wrong conclusion, and shared it with you. That shouldn't have happened."

Emma remembers a quote that she read somewhere: *As human beings, we suffer from an innate tendency to jump to conclusions, to judge people too quickly.*—Prince Charles

Emma is still quiet and gives them a wave as she turns down the walkway to her house. She is lost in her thoughts about Jimmy and everyone jumping to incorrect conclusions about Eve. She feels badly for her part in the situation and wonders if she should talk to her parents about the past few days' activities. *What would they feel and think about all of this?* Their feelings are still pretty raw, as far as Jimmy is concerned, too. She knows that they love both of their children very much.

THIRTEEN

PARENTAL CONFERENCE

Jen and Layla let themselves into their house as usual and begin to do their homework. Layla has vocabulary words to work on today. Jen scans the list of work she needs to complete and decides that she will get the kitchen ready to prepare dinner once their mother gets home. She will do her homework after dinner.

Robin had mentioned to Jen in the morning that tonight's dinner would be tacos. *Yum, Taco Tuesday!* Ground beef with refried beans, Spanish rice, and guacamole with chips are always welcomed by the Benson family.

Jen takes the cheese out of the refrigerator and begins to grate it. Next, she shreds the lettuce and chops tomatoes into small cubes. Robin comes in from work and is pleasantly surprised that Jen has already begun to prepare dinner. She goes to the refrigerator, takes out the ground beef, then grabs a frying pan from the cupboard and begins to cook. She adds a packet of McCormick Taco Seasoning, stirring as the meat becomes brown. The delicious aroma of the blended meat and seasoning reaches Jen and she smiles.

"Thank you so much for starting dinner, Jen," Robin says as she lovingly puts her hand on Jen's back.

"Oh, you're welcome, Mom." Jen obviously loves making her mom happy.

"Layla, how is your homework coming?" Robin asks.

"I'm almost done," Layla says with a little sigh.

"Could you please set the table for me?

"Sure, I will, Mommy," Layla says as she goes over to Robin and hugs her.

Layla takes the silverware from the drawer to the dining room table and places it at each family member's setting then goes back for the plates. Tonight, they are using Layla's favorite. The blue ones with the pretty daisy print. She loves how they look like someone has painted the three flowers on each plate, two with yellow centers and one with light blue.

"All done, Mommy!" she shouts.

Jeff has been working late these past couple of days. He is finally home, and dinner is on the table waiting. The Benson family sits down in their normal places. Usually, Jeff likes to ask how everyone's day has been once they all have their dinner on their plates. Robin puts the food on Layla's plate for her while Jen and Jeff serve themselves. Jen wants to get a jump on the "How did everybody's day go?" question tonight. She wants to tell her parents all about Eve and the adventures of the past few days.

"Mom and Dad, I have something that I want to tell you," Jen begins the conversation.

Hearing a teenage daughter saying that she has something to tell is a bit unnerving for any parents, but both Robin and Jeff remain quiet. Jeff nods for Jen to continue with what she has to say.

"Do you remember that I was sick at school a little over a week ago?" Jen asks.

"Yes," Jeff says calmly, despite his growing anxiety about what Jen might reveal. He nods his head indicating for Jen to go on as he takes a bite of his taco.

"Well, something that I didn't tell you at the time is that I overheard Ms. Heather talking to a girl who said that she was *high*."

"Really? Someone is doing drugs at your school?" Jeff asks, nearly spitting his food out.

"Well, that's what we thought too. I mean I told Emma and Kendall about it."

Robin sets her taco down on her plate. Then she asks, "What do you mean, that's what you thought?"

"After I told Kendall and Emma, we decided to try to find the girl. Of course, Emma is the most upset."

Jeff knows the Perez family well. He says, "I'm sure that she is," and with a slight pause, then adds, "but how did you know where to look for her?"

"I saw her last name on Ms. Heather's clipboard before I left her office. So, we started by looking through old yearbooks, but couldn't find her there. We did a Google search too with no luck. Then when Kendall was reading about the celebrities and other famous people Layla said that she knew someone named Connie Greene."

"So, your little sister is involved in this too?" Robin asks with a scowl on her face.

"Well, she is, but she isn't. She only helped us find out the girl's first name."

Layla fidgets in her seat. She wants to say something too because they are talking about her, but she does not know what to say. She can see that their mom is scowling at Jen, and she doesn't understand why. She thinks that she should be quiet in case she and Jen are in trouble and continues to eat her taco.

"Well, go on then," Robin tells Jen.

"So, once we knew her name, Kendall asked a boy who's in the junior class if he knows her. He doesn't, but he said that Kyle had recently met her."

"Now who is Kyle and how is he involved?" Robin asks shaking her head. She knows that teenagers sometimes get carried away with stories, rumors, and gossip, but she is a little worried about how far this situation has gone.

"Oh yeah, Kyle is Kendall's Youth Group Leader at their church and he has actually been very helpful. He talked to Eve and then set up a meeting for us all at Robinson Park today after school. And it turns out that Eve has type 1 diabetes."

Robin and Jeff remain quiet, trying to take it all in. Robin thinks ... *Okay, our daughter overheard a conversation and jumped to the wrong conclusion. She involved her friends and Layla as well. However, it now seems there has been a good outcome to the situation.*

"Mommy, may I have another taco?" Layla asks Robin, breaking into her thoughts.

"Of course, you may, Sweetie," Robin replies as she takes Layla's plate and adds a taco to it.

"More beans too?"

"No, thank you," Layla replies shaking her head.

Jeff asks, "So Eve is a diabetic, do you know exactly what that means?"

"Yeah, now we do. Eve said that she has to use a glucometer, do tests before and sometimes after she eats, and she wears an insulin pump all of the time," Jen answers, feeling proud of herself to have mastered the medical terms.

"That sounds like it would make her a lot different from your other classmates," Robin says.

"Yeah, Eve said that too. She said that she just wants to fit in and be like everybody else. We really feel badly that we almost accused her of doing something wrong. We want to try to make it up to her."

"Have you thought about how you could do that?" Robin asks.

"It's good that you see that you are the ones who have done something wrong and that you want to correct it," Jeff states as he reaches for another serving of tacos, beans, and rice.

"Well, we have talked about asking Eve to go to the movies or to get a treat at MacKenzie's Ice Cream. Probably the movies would be the best. But we need to figure out how to invite her. I doubt that Hallmark makes 'We're sorry we accused you of using drugs' invitations," Jen says with a little smirk on her face.

Jen feels a huge weight is lifting off her shoulders now that she is telling her parents everything. It always seems to feel better to her when her parents know what she has been stressed about, like the time that everyone thought that Mr. Jackson was going to move away and not be their teacher anymore. Her parents had listened to her concerns and told her that everything would work itself out. It is going to be the same for this situation too.

All we have to do is give a sincere apology to Eve and everything will be okay.

Once everyone has had their fill of the delicious Taco Tuesday dinner Jen and Robin clear the table, rinse the plates, and put them into the dishwasher. Meanwhile, Jeff is going over the vocabulary homework with Layla.

"Remember last week we had the word 'friend?'" Jeff asks Layla.

"Yes, Daddy, and Kim really is my friend," Layla replies with a big smile.

"Is Kim in your class?"

Layla does not answer, she merely nods indicating yes.

"Daddy, sometimes I hear you call your co-workers characters, but they don't wear costumes like the people at Disneyland."

"No, they don't. It just means that I think their actions are funny," Jeff explains.

"Okay, girls let's get into your pajamas and get calmed down. One TV show and it's off to brush your teeth, read and get to bed," Robin announces.

Layla is still confused about what is going on with Jen. She hesitates but thinks better of it because she thinks that she may have missed getting into trouble earlier at the dinner table. She goes into her room and puts on her soft, warm pajamas.

Jen goes to her room, feeling a lot more relaxed. She puts a CD in the player and listens as she changes from her regular clothes into pajamas. She lets her jeans and shirt stay on the floor where she drops them. Her mouth still feels a little hot from the tacos so she decides to brush her teeth.

Once the girls have their pajamas on, they go to the living room where Jeff and Robin are sitting.

"How about we watch something amusing tonight?" Jeff asks, thinking of how heavy the dinner conversation had been.

"Oh, that sounds great; I think we need to laugh," Robin responds having the same thoughts as Jeff.

"There are some good shows on Netflix," Jen adds.

They chose a comedy about a family that is like their family, except it is an older brother and a younger sister. They laugh and relax. Layla grows tired before the show is over. She keeps herself awake by stretching every few minutes.

"It's time to get into bed, Layla," Jeff says once the program has ended.

Jen and Layla each give their mom and dad a kiss and a hug and go to their rooms. As she lies on her bed, reading, Jen thinks about how to invite Eve to go to the movies. Maybe she, Kendall, and Emma could make an "I'm Sorry Invitation."

Robin asks Jeff to turn the television off. They both think that Jen has acted like the typical teenager in the situation and are happy with the way it has turned out so far. They always like to allow their children the freedom to figure things out for themselves even when it means that they will make mistakes. They believe that mistakes are necessary for the learning process.

"I was a bit skeptical when Jen said that she had something to talk to us about," Jeff says.

"I was too," Robin replies. "Jen is intelligent. Remember that quote? The one that says something like *"Intelligence is being able to learn from your mistakes; Wisdom is being able to learn from the mistakes of others."*

Jeff says, "Sure but, I'm curious as to how it will turn out with this apology movie event."

"Oh, I'm sure that it will be fine."

FOURTEEN

LET'S GET CREATIVE

Wednesday is a typical school day with classes, lunch, more classes, and the ringing of the final bell. The girls have decided to make an invitation for Eve to go to the movies. While sitting at Jen's dining room table they use colored construction paper, colored pencils and markers, glue, and some shiny confetti-like materials.

"Should we say that we are sorry first?" Jen asks.

"I think that she knows that we are sorry so maybe we should start with, 'You are invited to a movie.' I think that keeps it more positive," Emma replies.

"Sure, that sounds all right," Kendall says.

On white paper, Emma draws a flower. Not just any flower, but a daisy.

"We can use the yellow paper for the center of this and maybe turquoise or light blue for the petals," she says, as she proudly holds the page up for Jen and Kendall to see.

"Oh, that's going to be beautiful, Emma," Kendall says.

"Yes, I really like it. Of course, you are the artist!" Jen chimes in.

Jen then takes the scissors and cuts a circle from the yellow construction paper.

Kendall, who is very good at calligraphy, using the Lovely

Melody font because she thinks that it looks fancy, begins with: You Are Invited to a Movie.

"That looks almost professional," Jen says as she looks over Kendall's shoulder.

"I've seen this font in cards at the Hallmark store in the mall before," Kendall replies, matter-of-factly.

"Well, it's really lovely and I like it," Jen replies as she smiles and winks at Kendall.

Emma is drawing in the petals on her flower. Jen asks, "Are you going to use the cornflower blue or the turquoise for the petals?"

"I like the cornflower, but what do you think?"

"I like the turquoise," Kendall says.

"I like the other blue too," Jen adds.

"Well, then what if I use blue as the outline and turquoise for the center?"

"Sure," Kendall and Jen agree.

Emma picks up a dark blue colored pencil and outlines each petal. Then she reaches over for the turquoise pencil and starts to color each petal in. For a shadowing effect, she draws a few slightly curved lines in the middle of each petal with her dark blue pencil.

"Do we even know what movie we are going to see?" Jen asks.

"A romantic comedy might be the best. Or maybe something animated," Emma suggests.

They have not looked at the current movies that are playing at the mall. But there are always new movies coming out and usually there will be a light-hearted one for them to choose from. They want the movie to be enjoyable for everyone. Although they do not know Eve well enough to know what types of movies that she will enjoy, they think that she seems like a typical girl their age and they will be able to find one.

"We'll figure that out later," Kendall replies.

"We need to say that we will be paying for Eve's ticket on the invitation too," Jen states.

"Okay, I'm on it!" Kendall says.

Jen's mom comes home a little earlier than usual today. She finds them working on the invitation. Robin thinks that it looks good. On the left side is Emma's daisy with cornflower blue and turquoise petals, a yellow center, and a green stem with a leaf on each side all made with the various colored papers and pencils. To the right in red colored pencil are Kendall's words in the Lovely Melody calligraphy.

You are invited to a Movie
Saturday at 2 o'clock
At the Spectrum Mall
We've Got Your Ticket Covered

Jen gently places dots of glue around the card then she sprinkles glitter of various colors; red, blue, and silver over them.

"Hey Mom, what do you think of this now?" Jen asks as she holds the invitation up for Robin to see.

"Wow, that's pretty creative, girls!" Robin says with a smile.

"Great, I think that our work is done here!" Jen says with a look of satisfaction and pride.

The girls clean up the dining room table, putting everything away except the card which needs to dry. Kendall and

Emma stay for about a half-hour longer to work on their homework.

Meanwhile, Robin is in the kitchen preparing dinner. Tonight's dinner is baked stuffed pork chops, which she has purchased already stuffed at the butcher shop, with baked potatoes and mixed vegetables. She wraps the potatoes in aluminum foil, takes a baking pan from the cupboard, and puts the pork chops into it, pours barbeque sauce over them, then puts everything into the preheated oven. She then goes into the living room to sit and read the latest People magazine.

Before leaving for their homes, Emma and Kendall remind Jen not to forget the card when she leaves for school in the morning. They plan to find Eve before classes begin and give her the invitation which will give her time to think about it, as well as time to get permission from her mom to go if she decides to accept.

When Emma gets home, she decides to tell her parents what has been going on these past few days. She knows that she will have to ask for their permission to go to the movies if Eve accepts their invitation, so why not tell them everything?

Over dinner, Emma begins, "I have something that I need to tell you."

"Okay, what is it?" Julieta asks.

"I'm not even sure where to start."

"How about you start at the beginning?" Franco asks.

"Uhm, okay. So, Jen was sick at school a couple of weeks ago. Mrs. C sent her to Ms. Heather's office. She fell asleep for almost an hour. When she woke up, she overheard Ms. Heather talking to a girl who said that she was high."

"Someone is taking the drugs in your school?" Franco asks.

"No, but that's what we thought," Emma replies. "Anyway,

Jen had seen the girl's last name on Ms. Heather's chart. So, we tried to figure out who she was so that I could talk to her. Tell her about Jimmy, you know?"

"Yes, we understand that," Franco says. "But what happened next?"

After Emma went through all the details of their assumptions, their search for EG in yearbooks, on Google and through Layla's acquaintance with Connie, they looked at her seriously taking in all the information.

After a few minutes of silence, Julieta finally asks Emma, "You accused Eve of taking drugs but it turns out she has diabetes?"

"Yes, Momma, and we are all really sorry about jumping to the wrong conclusion, so we want to take Eve to the movies on Saturday as an apology," Emma replies with a bit of shame in her voice.

Then in a more excited tone, Emma says "But we made her an invitation today after school. So, is it all right if I go?"

"I think that would be a really good idea," Emma's mom speaks with some relief in her voice. "What do you think, Franco?" She turns to look at her husband who is scratching his chin.

"Yes, it is a good plan," Franco replies. "I see no reason why you shouldn't be able to go. Do you need some extra money to help pay for Eve's ticket?"

"Yes, please," Emma replies seriously, containing her happiness.

FIFTEEN

INVITING EVE

On Thursday morning, Jen, Emma, and Kendall arrive at school just a little bit earlier than usual. They walk to the other side of the main building and look around for Eve. They spot her wearing faded blue jeans, a light pink t-shirt with a cat printed on it, and her usual black Converse shoes. She walks toward them, acknowledging them with a nod of her head.

Jen is the first to speak. "Hi, Eve. We have something for you." As Jen gets Eve's attention, she reaches into her backpack and takes out their handmade invitation card.

"What is this?" Eve asks.

"We want to try to apologize for accusing you of … " Emma begins and trails off as she realizes other students are around and she does not want anyone else to hear what they have done. They are all sorry and embarrassed about their actions.

"I have to get to class," Eve replies coolly as she takes the card from Jen and puts it into her backpack.

"She seemed a little short. And we worked so hard on that card," Kendall says to Jen and Emma.

"Well, it is getting late, we only have about 2 minutes to get to class," Jen replies.

"See you later," Emma says as she heads towards her first class.

It is a usual school day, with classes, friends chatting as they walk through the halls, lunch, then the ever-beautiful sound of the ringing of the final bell.

After school, the girls look for Eve again. They find her in front of the school waiting for her mom to pick her up.

"Did you read our invitation?" Emma asks.

"I did, but I have to talk to my mom about it before I can give you an answer," Eve says as she gives them a half-smile.

"We understand. We all had to ask permission from our parents too," Jen says.

As the girls walk to Layla's school, Kendall says "Well, it seems like Eve is at least interested in going to the movies."

"Yeah, I hope that her mom says yes," Emma answers.

"I do too." Jen chimes in.

"Me, three," Kendall says with a smile.

Deanna passes Jen, Kendall, and Emma as she gets to the school to pick Eve up. Connie is already in the back seat. Eve opens the front door of their maroon van and climbs in.

Deanna smiles and asks, "How was your day?"

"It was okay," Eve replies hesitantly.

"Really, it was just, okay?" Deanna questions with a bit of concern.

"Yeah, did you see those three girls when you came in the driveway?"

"No, I didn't notice them. I was focused on looking for you. Who are they?"

"Well, it's a long story."

"So, tell me, we have time."

"Remember I told you about a week and a half ago that my glucose was super high all day?"

"Yes, I remember."

"Well, one of the girls, the one with the green shirt on," Eve says as she looks over her shoulder and back at the girls. "Her name is Jen."

"Hhmmm," Deanna replies, as she looks in the rearview mirror trying to see the girls.

"She was in Ms. Heather's office that morning sleeping because she had a stomachache. When she woke up, she heard me tell Ms. Heather that I was high. So, she thought that I was high on drugs."

"Oh, why didn't you tell me about this before?"

"I didn't want to worry you and I wanted to try to solve it on my own."

"Did you solve it?"

"Well, not all on my own. My new friend Kyle told me about them thinking that I was on drugs the other day and we met at the park to talk about it."

"Was that the day that you called me and asked to be picked up later?"

"Yes, then remember the next day you had the Teacher Conference for Connie?"

"I sure do."

"Well, that day Kyle had all of us meet at the park to talk. That's when I explained that I have diabetes. They all feel pretty bad about accusing me of something that I wasn't doing."

"So, you worked it out with them? And now they understand what having diabetes means?"

"Yeah, then today they brought me an invitation to go to the movies on Saturday as a 'we are sorry' kind of thing."

"Do you mean this Saturday?"

"Uh-huh, can I go to the movies with them, Mom, please?"

"Evie, give me a little while to think about it. We can talk again after dinner."

After picking up Layla, the girls walk home passing by the usual brown, turquoise, sage, and green houses along their way. It is a cool day and the shade from the trees makes it chilly. Kendall involuntarily shakes a little and she rubs her arms.

"What do you think Eve is going to tell her mom?" Jen asks.

"Do you mean is she going to tell her mom how stupid we were?" Emma asks.

"She will have to tell her why we are going to pay for her to go to the movies," Kendall says matter-of-factly.

"Yeah, I guess she will have to, won't she?" Emma asks.

"Do you think that her mom will allow her to go?" Jen asks.

"I don't know how she will react, but I don't think that my parents would be eager for me to hang out with people who have accused me of wrongdoing, would either of your parents?" Kendall asks.

"I hadn't thought about it that way," Emma replies.

"I think my parents would have to talk it over first," Jen says.

"My parents would be cautious," Kendall replies.

"I hope that Eve's mom doesn't see us as bad people. After all, we definitely are not. We made a mistake. We admitted it. We were concerned for *her* and we are trying to make up for it," Emma says a little more emotionally than she expects. "We are doing the right thing."

"Of course, we are good people, Emma," Jen insists.

"We just have to hope that Eve puts us in that frame when she explains everything to her mom," Kendall notes.

Once at home, Deanna tells Connie to go into the dining room to do her homework. Eve heads to her room to work on her assignments. She has US History to work on. Her class is studying the Civil War. She opens her textbook and begins to read.

Many causes lead to the American Civil War. While the most cited is slavery, other political and cultural differences between the North and the South contributed to the Civil War … .

<u>Industry vs. Farming:</u> The North no longer needed slaves, yet the South relied heavily upon slaves for their way of life.

<u>States' Rights:</u> Since the Constitution was written there have been arguments about how much power that states should have and how much the federal government should have.

<u>Expansion:</u> As the United States continued to expand westward … each new state became a battleground.

"Girls it's time for dinner," Deanna calls out breaking into Eve's reading.

"Coming!" Eve replies.

Deanna has made baked chicken breast, rice, and a blend of vegetables called Normandy, which has broccoli, cauliflower florets, sliced carrots, zucchini, and yellow squash. They sit around the dining room table to eat.

"Mom, have you decided if I can go to the movies on Saturday?" Eve asks as she reaches for a chicken breast.

"I've thought about it, and I think that it was a nice gesture for the girls to apologize that way. So yes, you may go."

"Oh, thank you! I can't wait to tell them tomorrow!" Eve excitedly declares.

SIXTEEN

SATURDAY AFTERNOON MOVIE

"It's Fri-yay, it's Fri-yay, whoo hoo, it's Fri-yay!" Jen sings to herself as she walks into the kitchen for breakfast. She goes to the freezer and takes out Eggos, pops them in the toaster, takes a plate from the cupboard, butter, and maple syrup from the refrigerator, and continues to hum her "Fri-yay" tune. She happily eats at the kitchen counter.

Layla is sitting at the dining room table eating, or rather playing with her food.

"Layla come on; we are going to be late!" Jen shouts in frustration.

"I'm coming!"

Jen and Layla meet Kendall and Emma, and begin walking to school.

"Do you think that Eve's mother said yes to her going to the movies with us tomorrow?" Emma questions.

"I hope that she did. I think that it'll be fun," Kendall replies.

"Yeah, it should be fun. I hope that she can go," Jen says. "I already picked out the movie. We're going to see the sequel *To All the Boys: P.S. I Still Love You.* I just loved the first one! Didn't you?"

"Yes! That's a great choice, and my dad said that he can drop all of us off at the mall," Emma offers.

"I hadn't really thought about how we were going to get there. That's nice of him," Jen replies.

"Here we are," Layla says as they arrive at her school.

"I'll see you this afternoon, kiddo," Jen responds.

Jen, Kendall, and Emma walk to the front part of their school where they had met Eve the previous day. They know that her mom drops her off in that spot and they're prepared to wait for her arrival. They have only been there a couple of minutes when the maroon van stops in front of them. Eve opens her door, turns to her mom for a kiss on her cheek, and gets out. The three girls encircle her with anticipation.

"Did you ask your mom if you can go tomorrow?" Jen is the first to ask.

"Yes, and she said that I can!" Eve excitedly replies.

"That's awesome!" Emma and Kendall chime in together.

Once they reach the school, the girls go their separate ways to their classes. Eve walks to Mr. Ebel's U.S. History class, while Jen and Kendall stroll to Mrs. Collins' English class and Emma is off to Mr. Mallet's room to help set up their Science Project.

⁓

When Saturday afternoon comes, Jen and Kendall walk to Emma's house since Mr. Perez has offered to drive the girls to the mall.

Jen decides to wear her jeans and ASU Sun Devils jersey that her Auntie Kel sent her just before the beginning of this school year. Auntie Kel had told her that a "sun devil" is a rainbow-like colored patch in the sky caused by the setting sun hitting patches of ice crystals at a high altitude. She also told her that sometimes they have "sun devil" weather in Phoenix. This is called a "haboob" which is a large, severe dust storm that happens in arid regions. There can be towering clouds of dust several miles high enveloping the world around you. They are not as scary as they look, because you get plenty of warning. About an hour before it hits, every cellphone in the Valley receives a text alert. Auntie Kel has joked that it's kind of like those movie scenes where a room full of government officials simultaneously get word of a developing disaster.

Kendall has selected a green vest—that brings out her eyes—over a long-sleeved white button-down shirt with khaki pants, a brown belt, and her brown leather shoes.

"Are you all ready to go to the mall?" Mr. Perez asks when he greets Jen and Kendall at their front door.

"Yes," Jen answers, then asks "Is Emma ready?"

"She'll be right out," Mr. Perez replies.

Emma is wearing navy blue cropped pants, a light blue tank top with a navy and white zig-zag pattern sweater, and black Converse high-top shoes.

The three girls get into the car, with Emma in the front seat and Kendall and Jen in the back. They drive through town to the mall. Mr. Perez pulls up to the front of the theater.

"I'll be back to pick you ladies up at 4:30," he says.

"Okay Dad, we will meet you here then," Emma says as she leans over and kisses his cheek.

"See you after the movie Mr. Perez," Kendall says as she and Jen get out of the car.

"Bye, and thanks for driving us here, Mr. Perez," Jen says.

The girls stand in front of the theater and wait for Eve.

Soon the maroon van pulls up and Eve gets out. They all walk together to the ticket booth. Eve reaches into her tan corduroy purse.

Jen holds a hand up and says, "No need, the invitation said that we have your ticket covered and we do."

"Oh, okay then."

After purchasing their tickets, they decide to sit at a table in the lobby. There is plenty of time; it is only 1:20 and the movie does not start until 2:00. Jen sits across from Eve who is wearing faded jeans and a beige shirt with a brown cardigan sweater over it. Kendall and Emma sit across from each other.

Eve starts the conversation. "You're Kendall, right?"

"I am definitely Kendall!" And they both break up laughing.

"And you are Emma?" Eve says, looking at Emma.

"That's me," she says with a smile.

"That's cool; I'm trying to get everybody's name right."

"And I'm Guilty-As-Charged Jen!" Jen says, then gets serious. "We are all here to express how sorry we are for what happened, as you know, and to get to know you better. We know that you moved here recently. Where did you move from?"

"We lived in College Place before we moved here," Eve replies. "It's just my Mom, Connie, and me."

"What about your dad?" Emma asks.

"He passed away a couple of years ago," Eve responds without missing a beat, so as not to have them feel sorry for her. "It was hard for me to leave my old school. I had been there since kindergarten. But my mom works here now so it was necessary. What about you guys?"

"We've lived here all of our lives, basically," Jen says. "We're all neighbors and have been for as long as any of us can remember." Quietly, she takes in the reality that this young girl not only has diabetes, but she has also lost her father.

"Let's get popcorn, candy, and sodas!" Kendall gushes.

"Can you even have soda and candy, Eve? I mean with the diabetes and all?" Emma blurts out.

"I'm good for now, I just ate lunch."

"Oh, okay," Kendall says, sounding a little disappointed.

There are a few minutes of silence and then Jen remarks, "So the other day you said that you had to carry your backpack with you everywhere you go. But today you're carrying a purse."

"I just got this the other day. I use it on the weekend because I don't have to have room for books and other school supplies," Eve answers.

She sets her purse down on the table. It looks like any normal purse that you might see at Target or any other department store. Eve unzips it and turns it over; bits and pieces fall out, a pen, Chapstick, a small hairbrush.

"So, this is all of my stuff," Eve says. She picks up a few of the everyday things. "My wallet, lip balm, hand wipes, tissues, some coins, all things that you probably have too. And here's my extra stuff." All three girls watch attentively.

"This is my extra bottle of insulin," Eve says as she holds up a small bottle. It is about half-full of a clear liquid.

"That's insulin?" Jen asks.

"Yup, do you want to hold it?"

Jen shrugs and Eve hands the bottle to her saying, "Just don't touch the top."

The top has a small metal cap with a rubber stopper in the center. "You can smell it if you want," Eve says. Jen sits looking at her with a skeptical expression.

Eve says, "Go ahead, it's okay."

Jen brings the bottle to her nose and draws in a breath then quickly holds it away. "Whoa!" she says, laughing.

"It stinks, doesn't it?" Eve asks as she too breaks out in an audible giggle.

"Yeah, it's kind of disgusting," Jen agrees while wrinkling her nose.

"I read that the smell is actually the preservative, I don't really know what insulin itself smells like," Eve quips.

Jen hands the bottle to Kendall while Eve holds up a red plastic case.

"This is glucagon," she says. "This stuff could save my life if I become hypoglycemic. That means my blood sugar or glucose level is too low. And if I cannot eat something quickly enough, I'll need this."

Eve opens the case. Inside is another bottle like the insulin bottle with a tiny white disk and a liquid-filled syringe. She takes the protective cap off the syringe and there is a good-sized needle attached.

"So, if I ever pass out, someone can take this syringe, put it in the bottle, push in all of the water and mix it with the little white disk. Then once the disk dissolves in the water, draw it back into the syringe and shoot it into me."

"But that needle is big!" Kendall says as she shudders.

"Yeah, I know, but I've never needed to use it before," Eve says as she covers the needle. There is a clicking sound and Eve puts the bottle back into the case.

"But since it's only useful for emergencies, like—say, for example, if I was to pass out, it doesn't really matter that much. I'd prefer a scary needle to the alternative!"

Eve passes the case to Emma who looks intently at the

instructions. There are pictures, no words. The last picture is of the needle being pushed into the thigh of a leg.

"You have to shoot that needle into your leg?" Emma asks with a quiver.

"Well, it shows a leg on there, but it could be in my arm or my butt," she says with a wink. "Except most of the time, when I feel like my glucose level is low, I can usually feel it coming on; I just eat some of these candies." She has several peppermints, butterscotch as well as some Tom & Jenny's Soft Caramels which she puts back into her purse.

"I'm sorry but I cannot share those."

"That's okay," Jen says. "They are kind of like your medicine. There is no sharing medicine. And your medicine is candy! How cool is that?"

Jen smiles while looking over at Emma. No sharing medicine has been one of Emma's points in her talks about Jimmy.

Eve continues, holding up a triple-A battery. "Here's my lithium battery for my pump, along with the supplies for it." She drops it into her purse and holds up a few clear bags, each has clear plastic on one side and paper on the other. She passes them around the table too. Jen is the first to ask what it is. Inside is a long string that looks kind of like fishing line.

"Well, that's actually two things. The tube is just a tube. The other thing is a cannula. It has a needle on it and I stick the needle in my stomach, pull it out, and leave the tube inside."

Both Kendall and Emma make displeasing faces.

Eve giggles and says "It's okay, really. It doesn't hurt to put it in and once it's inside, I hardly feel it there."

"So, what is this?" Emma asks holding up the other pack.

"Oh, that's called a cartridge. It holds the insulin and goes inside the pump. There's a big, fat needle in there that goes in the insulin bottle, but—thankfully, that needle never goes into me."

"Is this just a regular hand wipe?" Kendall asks holding up a small pack that looks like the wipes that they give you at the restaurant when you order a messy meal like BBQ Ribs.

"It may look like it," Eve responds. "But it isn't. It is an IV prep pad. It has alcohol in it, and some sort of sticky stuff that stays on your skin when you rub it on. When it dries, it gives the cannula something to stick to."

Then Eve stands up and reaches into her pocket and pulls out her pump. It has a thin tube coming out of one end which twists under her shirt and disappears. She sits back down and puts the pump on the table for the girls to see. She presses a button and the display lights up. It has the time in larger numbers and several words and other numbers.

"So, all day and all night, this pump pushes tiny spurts of insulin into me." Almost as if it was prompted; the pump makes a little *ssst ssst ssst* noise.

"Did you hear that?" All three of the girls nod. "That was it, just about every five minutes, it does that. It is doing what your bodies naturally do, which is to make small amounts of insulin all day and night, no matter what. This is called "basal" or sometimes "background" insulin. But whenever I eat, I must tell the pump how much I ate and it gives me an extra amount. That is called a "bolus" and is also known as "rapid-acting" insulin. It is to keep my blood sugar levels under control. You know, not too high and not too low."

There is one remaining item on the table. Jen points at it, "What's that for?"

"This is a glucose meter." Eve holds up a small, portable machine. "It's used to check my blood sugar levels. I need to prick my finger with this; it's called a lancet. Then I place a drop of my blood on this test strip, and it sucks it into the machine."

The meter (or monitor) soon displays the blood sugar level as the number, it is 123.

"That's not bad," Eve says.

"What number should it be?" Emma asks.

"Perfect is from eighty to a hundred and twenty. But for me, it is okay for it to be between seventy and one hundred and forty."

"Man," Jen says. "I thought that my life was chaotic with a little sister to look after every day and two working parents. But how on earth do you keep track of all of your stuff?"

Eve has a serious look on her face. "Hey, I didn't show and tell you all of this because I want your pity. This is my routine. I can do all the same things that you can. I can eat pretty much what I want. I just need to take a few extra steps than you do. I don't like it when people treat me differently. Just please treat me the same as you treat one another and I'll be fine."

Emma giggles and Eve looks over at her sternly. "What?" she challenges.

"It's just that I wasn't sure if we would like each other. But I really like you; you are 'high' spirited." She makes little quote marks in the air to engage the pun.

"I'd rather be 'high' spirited than just plain 'high!' Eve shows she can take a joke.

"I like you too!" Kendall says.

"Me, three," Jen chimes in.

Eve thinks for a few moments then replies, "Good, I like all of you too. You are inquisitive and most people are not.

They treat me like a 'diabetic' instead of a person. I'm not sure what that is since we are all different."

Emma looks at the clock on the wall and notes, "We only have five minutes; we had better get in there." They all dash over to the entrance, hand their tickets to the attendant, and hurry in to find their seats.

SEVENTEEN

AFTER THE MOVIE

On her way to pick Eve up from the movies, Deanna thinks about what it was like when Eve was first diagnosed with type one diabetes. Eve was five at the time she was diagnosed. There was no pump or CGM (continuous glucose monitoring). At that time, everything was manual.

A typical day included a morning check of her blood sugar level, then deciding what she would eat for breakfast and calculate the carbs, giving her the correct amount of insulin to offset those carbs. Next would be deciding what she would take to school for lunch, make it, pack it, and figure out the carb count then send her off to school. Before lunch, she would get her blood sugar level checked by the school nurse. The school nurse would give her insulin to cover lunch and correct her blood sugar level. Once she was home, it was time for a snack. First, check her blood sugar, then make the snack, next give her insulin. At dinnertime, check her blood sugar, make dinner, and give her insulin. Then there was bedtime, give her long-acting insulin (Lantus), tell her a story, and tuck her in. At 2 a.m., wake up and check her blood sugar. If needed, give her sugar or insulin. It was sort of like having a newborn again. One of the challenges was measuring all the carbs in what she ate, as well as making sure she ate all her food and that she did not grab any other food. It was a lot of management.

For Eve at five years old, it was terrifying; she had no idea what was going on. Nurses and doctors were coming at her with needles and IVs and she did not fully understand the urgency and why everyone was upset. It made her feel empty. She remembers asking if she was going to die. She thought she might because the first syllable of the word diabetes sounds like die. Even now, not a day goes by that fear does not rattle around in the back of her mind. At school, she was bullied for being different, told she was faking diabetes, or that she could not do or eat certain things.

Diabetes is a disease which causes your body to be at war with itself daily. You never know if your decisions are correct, if you will manage through the night, or if you will have complications; it goes on and on. Diabetes is a disease of science. There is no perfect way to control or manage it. Type 1 diabetics are warriors. They are strong, they are compassionate, and they are human.

Eve has shed many tears, experienced a lot of frustration, and defeat along with her advancements and all sorts of stuff in between. Diabetes is a tough disease, but it will never stop her. It has made her who she is today. Deanna is grateful for the medical advancements that have been achieved like the pump and CGMs. These devices have made a big difference in their lives. Eve often tells herself, "I may have diabetes, but diabetes doesn't have me."

☙

Once the movie finishes, the girls all dance out of their theater and down the hallway still singing *You Should Be Dancing*. Jen, Emma, and Kendall stop at the restroom. Eve continues to walk toward the exit door, she shouts, "I'll see you later, my mom texted that she is waiting for me out front. Thanks again for the movie. I had fun!"

All three girls reply, "You're welcome!"

☙

"Did you have a good time with your new friends?" Deanna asks as Eve gets into the van.

"Yes, and before the movie, I showed them all of the stuff I have to carry around with me," Eve replies with a smile.

"Hmmm, it sounds like it was fun and educational for them too," Deanna responds as she puts the van in gear and pulls out of the parking space.

Mr. Perez is in the parking lot when Emma, Jen, and Kendall come out of the movie theater. They see him parked in a space looking down at his phone and walk over to get into his car.

"Hey girls, was the movie a good one?" he asks.

"It was fun," Emma answers, "but learning about how Eve controls her diabetes was a lot more interesting than the movie."

"She has to carry a lot of stuff with her like an extra bottle of insulin which really stinks," Jen adds. "I mean, truly, it smells really awful."

"And she has a huge needle that can save her life if she becomes hypoglycemic; that means her glucose level is too low," Kendall pipes in. "But she said that she has never had to use it."

"She carries peppermint, butterscotch, and some Tom & Jenny's Soft Caramels in her purse in case she feels like her glucose level is getting low," Emma adds. "It's like her medicine."

"And hand wipes," Kendall says. "They look like the ones that you get at the restaurant when you order BBQ Ribs."

"All day and all night, her pump pushes tiny spurts of insulin into her," Jen says. "And the pump makes this little '*ssst ssst ssst*' noise."

"And don't forget about her glucose meter; it's a small machine used to check her glucose levels," Emma adds. "She has to prick her finger with something called a lancet, place a drop of blood on a test strip that gets sucked into the machine. Then the meter displays her glucose level as a number on the meter's digital display screen."

"Well, all that sounds very educational," Luis replies as they pull into their driveway.

"I'd better hurry up; I have the Homecoming dance with Jacob tonight!" Kendall says as she jumps out of the Perez car and hurriedly walks up the sidewalk, leaving Jen behind.

EIGHTEEN

JACOB'S HOMECOMING DANCE

Kendall goes straight to her room to get ready for her date. She is anxious to wear her new dress. The top is black chiffon with spaghetti straps. The skirt is red and flowing. It is above the knee length. She will match her dress with her black patent leather shoes. She and Jacob had talked about them both wearing white Vans, but Kendall has decided that the shiny shoes will be more fitting. Jacob will dress to match her. He will be wearing a red dress shirt with a black bow tie, black slacks, and as he had wanted, his white Vans.

Kendall thinks about how cute Jacob is as she brushes and curls her hair. *His smile with his braces is cute. His blond, but almost light brown hair combed with a bit of a wave is so cute. The way that Jacob is nearly a foot taller than me is also cute. Jacob is just so dang cute!*

She applies a small amount of liquid makeup, just enough to make her skin look slightly tanned. Then she applies a few strokes of black mascara. She chooses not to wear any eyeshadow. Next, she dabs a little *Sweet Like Candy* perfume on her neck. And lastly, she applies a light pink gloss to her lips.

Looking in the mirror she thinks, *Yep, I'm ready!*

"Are you going to have something to eat before we take you to the school?" Kate calls out to Kendall.

"No, I'm too nervous to eat anything."

The plan is for Kendall to meet Jacob at the school. He has said that he will wait for her in front of the gymnasium. He has two other friends and their dates who will be there too. Jacob's friends are all older than Kendall. But she does not care. Jacob has asked her to go to the Homecoming dance and she is going to go and have fun.

"We will be back to pick you up around 11:00," Liam tells Kendall as they pull up in the rear of the school. "Please wait right here."

"Don't be too nervous and have fun," Kate says as Kendall opens the car door and gets out.

"Okay, I will."

Kendall walks to the door of the gym and sees Jacob standing with his friends. He turns around and rushes to open the door for her. He walks over to her, smiling, and gives her a hug. He smells like a combination of *First Instinct* (Abercrombie & Finch cologne); somewhat citrusy and fruity with a hint of melon and Snuggle dryer sheets, fresh and clean. He seems even taller with his arm around her shoulder as he walks her over to the group. Jacob's friends greet Kendall with warm smiles.

"I really like your dress," Beth, Doug's date, says to Kendall. "Black and red is a good combo."

"You two match! How cute is that?" Kerry, Ryan's date chimes in.

Just then, Kendall notices that Jacob has a small box in his hand. Inside the box is a red rose with white baby's-breath corsage and a matching boutonniere. Although it is a tradition that the female brings the boutonniere neither Kendall nor Jacob care about that.

Jacob takes the corsage out of the box and, trying to make Kendall laugh, asks, "May I, my lady?"

Kendall nods in agreement and blushes a little. Jacob places the corsage on her left wrist.

She then reaches in and takes the boutonniere out of the box and with a smile begins to pin it to the left side of Jacob's shirt. Her hands are shaking a little bit. While she fumbles with the pin, Kerry snaps a photo of them on her iPhone.

As Doug takes Beth's arm in his, he says, "Well, you two look ready, let's go in."

Jacob takes Kendall's arm in his and they follow Doug, Beth, Kerry, and Ryan into the gym. To their left, as they walk through the door is a black cardboard Paris bistro silhouette. The table has an umbrella in the middle. A vase with flowers sits on the table.

"Did you know Paris is famous for its charming bistros and quaint cafés?" Doug asks in a tour-guide-like voice, as he looks at the group.

The wall at the far end of the gym has been covered in blue paper and a white full moon has been painted on it. To the right of the moon stands a beautiful golden Eiffel Tower. It is a little over 9 feet tall.

Throughout the room, there are strings of white lights. "It looks like pictures that I've seen of Paris," Kerry says as she twirls around once, taking in all the decorations.

To their right is the photo booth. "We should get the professional-type photos," Ryan says to the group, giving Kerry a little wink.

The group of six go over and stand together. The photographer takes several shots of them as a group and then a few more as couples, one shot of just the guys and another of just the girls and finally, a few more shots of the group using the props that have been provided. Beth uses the pink one that says "Merci" and has pretty, little hearts. Doug uses the black Eiffel Tower. Jacob uses a thick black mustache. While Kendall uses a black hat with a pink ribbon around it. Once they feel that they have taken every shot possible they all walk over to the food and drink table for punch and snacks. There are cookies decorated with "Paris," "Ooh, la, la," and, of course, some in the shape of the Eiffel Tower.

"Do you want to dance?" Jacob asks Kendall.

"Sure, why not?"

"They make such a cute couple," Beth bubbles.

"She is so young and really sweet," Kerry replies.

"Let's dance!" Ryan shouts over the music to Kerry.

Once out on the dance floor, Ryan and Kerry dance near Jacob and Kendall. Doug and Beth join in and as a few loud songs, such as "Burnin' Up" by the Jonas Brothers and "So What" by Pink play, they are singing and shouting to the music, which is so much fun.

Soon it is time for the crowning of the King and Queen. Doug and Beth are sure that Ryan and Kerry will be crowned, and they think just the opposite.

"Your nominees for Queen are Kerry Crawford, Beth Davis, Hannah Miller, and Tammy Williams. For King, the nominees are Marcus Hughes, Nick Young, Doug Wells, and Ryan Wilson. Now may I introduce our principal Mrs. Hunt who will announce the king and queen," the deejay announces.

"Thank you and good evening! I hope that you are all having a good time," Mrs. Hunt says as she opens the first envelope.

"Your new queen is Tammy Williams."

"And your king is Marcus Hughes."

"I was sure that one of you was going to win," Jacob says as he turns to face Beth, Doug, Kerry, and Ryan.

Beth speaks first, "It's fine."

"Yeah, it's okay with me too," Kerry says.

The deejay begins to play music again. As the night begins to wind down, he plays "Perfect" by Ed Sheeran. Beth and Doug stay and dance, gazing into each other's eyes. Ryan, Kerry, Jacob, and Kendall move off the dance floor to talk.

"It's getting warm in here," Jacob mentions. "How about we go outside, Kendall?"

"What time is it anyway?"

"It's 10:45."

"My parents will be here in fifteen minutes and I'm supposed to meet them in front."

"I'll walk you out there then," Jacob says with his usual smile.

The air is cool and Kendall did not think to bring a sweater, jacket, or even a simple shawl. She shivers a little.

"Should we just go back in and wait until we see your parents drive up?" Jacob asks.

"Yeah, that's probably a good idea."

Within a few moments, Liam and Kate drive up. Kendall is facing Jacob with her back to the door.

"I think that's your chariot, my lady," Jacob says with a wink and smile.

"I believe that you are correct, sir." Kendall curtsies, which cracks Jacob up.

"I had fun tonight," Jacob says smiling down at her.

"Yeah, I did too," Kendall says smiling up at him. Then she turns and walks out the door saying, "See you."

NINETEEN

A TOUR OF HISTORIC DOWNTOWN

For a few weeks, the girls plan to hang out with Eve. Yet something always seems to get in the way. Track meets for Kendall and family functions for Emma.

Finally, on a Friday morning, Jen announces, "My parents want to do the *Be a Tourist in Your Town* tour of Old Towne on Sunday. I have invited Eve, we should get to know her better, you know?"

"I have a church function to go to this weekend, and we leave right after school," Kendall replies.

"This Sunday is not good for me either. We have a late lunch with family," Emma says.

"Um, okay, I guess it will be Eve and my family then."

When Sunday arrives, Jen and Layla wake up to Jeff and Robin making a big breakfast of eggs, bacon, fried potatoes, and sourdough toast. There will be many things to see on their walking tour. Jen holds the flyer and reads aloud to the family over breakfast about the sites that they will see in Old Towne.

"The tour starts at the County Courthouse which was built in 1929 in the Spanish Colonial Revival style. This building features a beautiful, blue-tiled dome and an elegant courtyard. The east wall of the presidio is marked with a granite strip in the red tile walkway inside the courtyard. An actual piece of the original presidio wall can be seen in the assessor's office on the south side of the courtyard."

"The second stop is the Mormon Battalion Sculpture, a bronze statue that commemorates the day in 1846 when Mormon soldiers entered the city on their way to California to fight in the Mexican War. The Spanish-speaking citizenry, despite their rattled nerves about these armed outsiders, treated the soldiers to a fiesta. One of the Mormon soldiers joined in the fun by playing his fiddle. Note you can see his fiddle case on the north side of the statue."

Layla begins to giggle at how "official" Jen sounds. "*You* should be the tour guide!" she laughs.

Robin sends Layla a brief smile while waving her hand to be quiet, and nods to Jen to continue. "Then onto the *Soldado De Cuera* which means the Leather Jacket Soldier Sculpture. He is a Spanish soldier that stands in the battle uniform typical of the late 1700s. The leather vest (7 layers of rawhide) could stop an arrow. The leggings protected him from thorns. His shield helped to deflect arrows and his 10-foot-long lance was the premier weapon of the day."

"If you memorize this Jen, you will be the Superstar of Old Towne!" Robin says between bites of toast. Jen smiles before she goes on, sounding more official with every word.

"Our fourth site is to cross the Allande Footbridge; this bridge crosses Pennington St., which is dedicated to Don Pedro de Allande y Saabedra who was appointed one of the first commanders of the presidio in 1777. Allande personally financed the early construction efforts at the presidio, which was the largest in the Southwest."

"Then over to Garces Footbridge; this bridge crosses

Broadway. It commemorates Father Francisco Garcés, the Franciscan priest who rode north from Tubac with Lt. Col. Hugo O'Conor in 1775 to find the Presidio. He explored throughout the region and died in 1781."

By this time, Layla and Jeff were all winking at each other, chuckling at how serious Jen was presenting the tour. Yet it seemed there was no stopping her!

"Our sixth stop is the Gazebo in Plaza De Mesilla. It is a replica of the original 1880s bandstand in the plaza and is the site where the stagecoach would gallop into town from Mesilla, New Mexico, or San Diego along the old El Camino Real (the Royal Road). Often, Apache arrows are embedded in the stagecoach from encounters along the trail. La Placita, as it is called now, is a collection of shops and offices that were built in the 1970s on the site of an old neighborhood as part of urban renewal."

"Next, we see the Francisco "Pancho" Villa Statue. Looking through the wrought iron fence we will see a commanding statue of Pancho Villa on the grassy area in the center of Broadway. The statue was given to the city by Mexico in 1981, with a wry sense of irony, considering Pancho Villa made outlaw incursions into the state."

Jen looked up and paused to take a sip of orange juice. Layla had finished her breakfast, and knowing she should be polite, was trying not to fidget in her chair.

"Our eighth stop is at Sosa-Carrillo-Fremont House. This house museum was once owned by the Sosa-Carrillo families; the oldest part of the structure was built early in the 1850s." Jen continued, "It was briefly used as the residence of members of the family of General John C. Frémont, who was appointed the Territorial Governor in 1878. This Sonoran row house contains an excellent example of a zaguán, a central hall, leading from the front to the rear yard. The mission fig in the courtyard was probably planted in the 1700s. To the west, we will see a basaltic peak. This was once a lookout for Spanish and Native American sentinels, who watched for raiders approaching the presidio and mission. The Tohono O'Odham name for the mountain, pronounced Schook-schon, means 'at the black base.'"

"Now on to Teatro Carmen. This is an adobe building with an interesting and checkered history, named for the wife of its builder, Carmen Soto Vásquez, it opened on May 20, 1915, as a theater devoted to staging dramatic works in Spanish. Carmen brought in plays from Spain, operas, dramas; both historic and contemporary. By the early 1920s, however, movies and boxing matches were more popular. Teatro Carmen closed to reinvent itself as a movie theater, dance hall, and boxing arena. It was sold in 1926 and became a garage. Its exterior was featured in the movie *Boys on the Side* in 1995."

"The tenth stop is Ferrin House (now The Coronet); it's an old adobe home that was built in the 1860s by tailor Joseph Ferrin and his wife Therese. A store was added to the residence in the 1880s; the structure now operates as a family-owned restaurant. Therese and her daughter Clara were also instrumental in building the first synagogue in the state on south Stone Ave."

"That would be a great place to end for a late lunch," Jeff declares.

"All right then, let's get these dishes into the dishwasher and head out," Robin adds.

Relieved that they are finally on their way, Layla jumps out of her chair and takes the plates to the kitchen. Robin rinses the dishes and Jen loads them into the dishwasher. Jeff takes a light jacket from the hall closet for Layla and asks Robin and Jen if they need anything.

"I think that we will be fine," Jen says.

∾

Deanna's van pulls up in front of the Benson's house. Eve leans over and kisses Deanna on the cheek and says, "I'll text you when we are on our way back."

"Okay, have fun and listen to Jen's parents."

Eve acknowledges her request with a nod, gets out of the van, and walks over to the Benson's car.

"Hi everybody!"

"Hi Eve!" the Bensons say in unison.

"Are you ready for an adventure?" Jen asks Eve.

"I sure am!" Eve says as they all get into the car.

"Is everybody buckled in?" Jeff asks, putting the car in reverse to back out of the driveway.

"We are all ready, Daddy!" Layla says with excitement in her voice.

The morning and early afternoon are going pretty much as the flyer that Jen had read during breakfast until Layla spots a wall with crosses, vases of beautiful flowers, and candles.

Tugging on Jen's hand and pointing she asks, "What is *that*?"

Jen pulls the flyer out of her back pocket. "Oh, that's the Wishing Shrine."

"I don't remember you reading about that," Robin says.

"I must have missed that, it says *One legend associated with this shrine involves a tragic love triangle in the 1870s, with a husband killing his wife's lover. A priest would not let the man be buried in the consecrated cemetery so local people lit candles at this location to pray for his soul."*

"Wow, that's an interesting, but kind of scary story," Eve says.

Once at The Coronet, they need to decide what to eat. The menu has a nice lunch variety.

"Do you want the seared chicken breast with broccolini or maybe the Kinder Cheeseburger with the cucumber salad?" Robin asks Layla once they are all seated.

"I think I want the Kinder Cheeseburger, but you know that I don't like mayo on burgers very much."

"Okay, we can ask them not to put mayo on it. Are you okay with the cucumber salad?"

"Yes, I like cucumbers."

"Would you like to try a Temple Devine for your drink?"

"What is that Mom?"

"It is lemon-lime soda with a splash of red syrup that is a little sweet and a little sour."

"Okay. I'd like a Temple Devine then."

"I'd like the seared chicken breast with the roasted root vegetables from the adult menu and could I start with a blueberry, kiwi, and pear salad, please?" Jen asks once Layla has expressed her choice to Robin.

"I'm going to copy you," Eve says looking at Jen.

"That sounds really good," Jeff responds. "I may have that as well."

"Well, I think that I'm going to go with the grilled pork chop and whipped sweet potatoes. The blueberry, kiwi, and pear salad—to start with—sounds really yummy too," Robin says.

"And I'd like to try the Cat's Meow to drink, please," Jen adds. "No wait I would rather have the Daisy Chain, it has peach, chamomile, and lemon and sounds refreshing."

"May I have the Cat's Meow?" asks Eve.

"Sure," Robin answers.

"Do you want a cocktail, Robin?" Jeff asks.

"No, I'm going to stick with something non-alcoholic. The Daisy Chain sounds good to me."

"All right, I'm going to have a Guinness draught."

Once they have decided on their lunch choices, they close their menus to signal their server that they are ready to order.

Jen feels that she and Eve are becoming friends. She wants to hang out with Eve more. *We can visit the museum. We can have a board game night. Kendall and Emma can bring over their favorite games, we could draw out of a hat to decide which to play. We can have a frock swap. We'll gather all the clothes we never wear. We will put them all in a pile, then take turns pulling pieces out to try on. We would all leave with new-to-us clothes, and they will all be free! There must be a ton of adventures that we can go on. It's really wonderful when something good can come out of something troubling. I love having Eve as my new friend.*

ACKNOWLEDGMENTS

Thank you to Dallas Woodburn—my friend, my Miranda Bailey, and Olivia Pope (rolled into one)—for your countless hours of instruction, emails, and many face-to-face conversations. Without you, my words would not have left my head and landed on these pages. I am forever grateful to you.

Thank you to Deborah DeNicola, my copy editor extraordinaire, for so many encouraging words and suggestions. You are kind, caring, and thoughtful about my work. As a writer, you know how much blood, sweat, and tears I have put into my baby. I could not ask for a better person to work with in bringing this book and its characters to life! I thank my lucky stars that I was able to find you!

I would to like thank editorial director Anne Stanton of Mission Point Press for her patience and support throughout this process.

Thank you to Jackie Denis, my copy and line editor, for your insight and clarification of medical issues that I needed to address. You were spot on.

Thank you to Kristen Rose, my beta reader, for your encouragement to expand in areas needing more details. I am also grateful for your enthusiasm about the cover artwork and for your suggestion to write a sequel. We will have to see if these characters continue to speak to me.

Thank you to Sheila Lowe. Yes, that Sheila Lowe, author of the Claudia Rose forensic mystery series! You inspired me to create my own mystery for teens.

Thank you to Andrew Kinser, for designing my cover. I truly appreciate your unflappability and creativity.

Thank you to Jonathan Arlia, my headshot photographer for your ingenuity.

Thank you to my girls, Kellie and Rebecca, for your constant love and support. I will let you decide which of these teens best embodies each of you.

Thank you to Hank, my husband, for your love, encouragement, and for patiently listening to me read this to you in my teenage voice(s). Thank you for proofreading this work. Without your support, I would not have been able to bring this book to life. You are my everything; you make each day an adventure.

Elaine Clark Aldrete was born in Claremont, New Hampshire, lived for many years in Santa Paula, California, and currently resides in Tucson, Arizona. A dedicated mother, wife, businessperson, and instructor, she became an avid volunteer in Ventura County, California. She served as a board director for the nonprofits Diabetes Explorer Educational Foundation, Inc. and Grants to You. She also volunteered for the latter nonprofit as an instructor and Ventura County director.

In 2012 Elaine founded Teaching Life Choices, Inc., a nonprofit devoted to captivating and engaging the minds of children to learn, have fun and make good life choices. To learn more, go to www.teachinglifechoices.org. Author of *Does Diabetes Mean You Die* published for young elementary students, *G-R-E-E-N-E* is her debut middle-grade book. Both books strive to inspire a greater sense of empathy and awareness, a mission of her nonprofit.